Rescued by Christmas

Marilyn Conner Miles

Marilyn Conner Miles

EXCERPT FROM RESCUED BY CHRISTMAS

"Well, as I see it, you have two options. You can either make up some excuse and tell Dane you can't ride to and from work with him anymore and stop worrying about getting caught, or tell him the truth."

"I–I can't."

"Why not? Are you worried his family will take the horse away? I know you've always wanted one."

"No...well yeah, that too, but that's not it."

"Are you worried about how you will get to work—though why you moved somewhere so far out in the country that it doesn't have bus service, I don't get." She shook her head

"No...although yeah, that is a problem right now without my car...But that's not it."

"Are you afraid you won't see him anymore if you don't have a reason to see him every day? By the way, I can't see that happening. From all you've told me, this guy likes you, Micah."

"That's the problem! I like him too. And if I tell him what I've been doing, sneaking around because I'm not supposed to have anything to do with him, what will he—and his family—think of me? They have a business too. They would expect their employees to follow the rules. At first, I did ride with him because I trusted him and I needed a way to get to work, that's true, but now—"

"Now, you don't know how to tell him the truth without losing him," Jasmine finished for me.

I nodded.

"But you're risking losing your job, and girlfriend, you really need this job."

"I know."

Marilyn Conner Miles

Dedication:
To caregivers of people and animals—and to all our rescued pets, large and small

Acknowledgement:
Pat Brown and Lori Harris who founded the Adopt-A-Horse program, Wilma Tronstad and Michelle Miner who founded Ripley's Horse Aid Foundation, the Clark County Executive Horse Council who sponsors them, and the many foster caregivers and professionals who care for the rescued horses of Clark County in Washington State.

Look for Marilyn Conner Miles's other titles
Acapulco Adventure, Holiday Heart, Perfect Pair, Saddle Up For Love, Belle's Christmas

Copyright © 2016 Marilyn Conner Miles

All rights reserved.

ISBN-13:978-1540335760

ISBN-10:1540335763

CHAPTER ONE

I knew I was no longer in control when my car began to slide down the hill. The steering wheel just seemed to take over. No matter how hard I tried to regain control and wrestle it away, the car acted as though it had a mind of its own. When it drifted to the left toward the yellow lane divider stripe, I let up on the gas pedal, made one last white-knuckle effort and watched as if in slow-motion, as my car slowly drifted the other way. Thank goodness there were no other cars on the road.

I could barely suppress my panicked feelings. But I told myself I needed to calm down and keep going. I couldn't be late for my first day on the job. If I could just get down to the bottom of the hill, everything would be fine. After my heartbeat slowed, keeping the car as close to the curb as possible, I let the tires bounce off it a little and slowly progressed down the hill. I knew it was hard on the tires, but it kept the car moving without spinning out.

I'd nearly reached the bottom, when I saw the

large red stop sign on a snow-speckled post, almost in front of the hood of my car. I'd concentrated so hard on just getting down the hill, I hadn't thought about what I'd do when I got there. Maybe I could just keep going through the intersection without stopping. No such luck, I saw a behemoth jacked-up monster pickup truck, approaching from the cross street on the left. No way could I get through the intersection before it got there. It was coming up way too fast. As it passed, its big tires sprayed dirty snow across my windshield.

I'd been so anxious to leave home and get on the road this morning, I'd cleared snow off just the hood, and windows. I drove slowly, but as soon as the car went faster than a crawl, big clumps of the cold white stuff flew off the roof onto the windshield. It had been difficult to see before, but when they were filthy as well, it made visibility even worse.

I saw another car approaching, this time from the right. It looked pretty far away. With much more confidence than I'd felt since I left my driveway, I stepped on the gas pedal, prepared to shoot across the road.

The car seemed to hesitate, so I stepped harder on the gas, felt the car slip a little, then it flew across the intersection. I caught a brief glance at the shocked face of the other car's male driver before my car slid off the road—and took a nosedive into a ditch.

I'd hoped if I started out early before the roads got too crowded, it would ensure I got to work on time. Of course, no one was stupid enough—or desperate enough—to drive in this weather, and down the hill—except me.

Maybe no one else was starting a new job in Clarkville that day either, the only reason I'd even attempted to drive in six inches of pristine snow on an unplowed rural road. It hardly ever snowed west of the Cascade Mountains in November. In fact, in my thirty-five years, I could probably count the times on one hand and still have fingers left over. So why that day of all days?

I fumbled around in my purse for my cell phone, but when I didn't find it, realized that in all my haste, I'd left it on the charger by my bed.

I couldn't just sit there, even though it was much

warmer than outside. I needed to at least *try* to flag someone down, although really, what were the chances that someone would stop by to help? The few drivers who ventured out were probably as anxious to get to work on time as me, without stopping to help a woman whose car had plowed into a ditch.

Gingerly, I pushed the door open, afraid to rock the car. It scraped the ground and stopped at about six inches. With my heavy winter coat on—which I wasn't about to take off—no way could I squeeze through. I shoved harder. *Stuck.* Not only was there a lot of it, but the snow was wet and heavy, not the light, fluffy stuff. And it must have frozen during the night after it snowed, because when I put my foot out on the ground, it slipped. I hastily pulled it back and shut the door, shivering.

Great. Not only was my car stuck precariously in a ditch, but I couldn't get the door open wide enough to get out. And if even I could, it was probably too icy to stand on the shoulder of the road. But that left me in the same predicament. I needed to let my boss, the executive director, know why I'd be late. I sighed.

Just when my funds were nearly depleted, after

weeks—actually *months*—of looking for work, I'd finally landed a job, moved almost 180 miles to this small town and found a place to live. I'd even splurged on the winter coat, anticipating my first paycheck. But now, there might not even *be* a job, and who knew what kind of costly damage to my car. I wanted to cry. Instead, I banged my hand on the steering wheel in frustration.

Ouch!

I was so wrapped up in my pity party, it took me a few minutes to register the noise I heard outside my car. Twice, I'd heard cars slowly pass by, and held my breath each time, hoping they would stop. I told myself that they just didn't see my car, or maybe thought it was abandoned. This time, though, someone stopped. Through the snow-covered back window, I could just barely see a man on the other side of the ditch, probably trying to determine if anyone was actually in the car.

I pushed on the door and opened it enough to call to him. "Can you help me? I can't get out. The door is stuck!"

After a couple minutes, I felt a tug on it as though he wanted to see for himself. I let go of it just in time, because after another tug, I heard a loud scraping, grinding sound and the door opened at least a foot.

"Ma'am, do you think you can get out now?"

Ma'am? Well, I supposed he hadn't seen me, just heard my voice, since I couldn't see him either. "Yes, I think so, but will it make the car slide forward more?" I asked anxiously

He laughed and then seemed to realize it might not be a laughing matter to me. "Sorry, uh, no, I wouldn't worry about that. Your car can't move any farther. Here, grab my hand," I heard him say.

"Oh." If I'd known that, I might have tried a little harder to get out. "I'll try." I swiveled in the seat and stuck one foot out and then the other. I looked at the space between the shoulder and the ditch and wondered how I'd get out of the car, up the ditch and onto terra firma without jerking him off his feet. "Okay, here goes."

"Don't worry, I've gotcha," he said. I could see his legs braced and he'd clasped my right hand with both of his.

I clutched the armrest with my left hand and awkwardly pushed off the seat. My feet slipped on the snow, but I dug in my heels and launched myself across the ditch...smack into my rescuer's arms.

I clung to him for an awkward moment while I caught my breath. I couldn't help thinking how nice it felt to be in a man's arms again. But only for a moment. He was a total stranger, though a kind one, who came through like a knight in shining armor when I needed help.

Though I am fairly tall for a woman at five foot eight, he had to be over six feet. I craned my neck to look up at him briefly, and my heart skipped a beat. He was very attractive, about my age I guessed, with large, bright blue eyes. And though I couldn't see his hair color under a wool navy watchman's cap, I noticed he had a short, reddish-brown beard flecked with snow. Embarrassed, I let go of him as soon as I could stand without falling.

"Have you called for a tow truck?" he asked.

"Uh, I...no, "I answered, still thinking about the 'hug.' I mentally shook myself. "No, I–I don't have a cell phone with me." He probably thought I was a totally unprepared idiot.

"Well, you can use mine if you want, but we

shouldn't stay here. It's too dangerous."

We both turned at the sound of a loud *bang* and then a *crunch* as two cars slid into each other coming down the hill my car crept down earlier. I understood what he meant. If my car slid off the road, others could too.

"Where were you headed when this happened?" He gestured to the ditch.

"To work. It's my first day at my new job."

He looked at me as though waiting for me to continue.

"Oh. Golden Valley. It's a retirement community on—"

"Yes, I know where it is. My grandfather is in the nursing care wing. In fact, I was on my way there too. I visit him every morning before work. How about if I give you a ride while you call a tow truck?"

I hesitated. I'd never accepted a ride from a stranger in my life, something my parents drilled into my head when I was younger. Could I trust him? He *had* helped me. And he visited his grandfather every day. Who did that? No one *I* knew. Besides, if I went with him now, I might actually get to work in time. I decided to take the chance.

I guess I hesitated a little too long.

"By the way, my name is Dane Andersen," he said. "My parents wanted to name me after my grandfather, but he wouldn't let them. He was afraid they'd call me Third or Trey or something like that. My grandpa is proud of his Danish heritage, so Mom compromised. Hence, my name."

"Yeah, well that's not so bad. My name is Micah McMillan. I got named after my dad, Michael. I guess they expected a boy. Dad suggested they name me Mike, but Mom wouldn't go for that, so *she* compromised and named me Micah. Not M-i-k-a, either—I guess in case someone mistook the 'a' for an 'e'—but M-i-c-a-h. Still looks like Michael. Boy, did that make it hard to find anything with my name on it. You know, all those cute things they have for kids, like license plates for your bike, or pencils or souvenirs? Stuff like that."

"Yeah, I got called 'Great Dane' a lot in school."

I smiled at him in commiseration, but then I heard him jiggling the keys in his hand and remembered I hadn't answered his question. "Yes, please, I'd appreciate a ride to work."

By car, it wasn't too much farther to Golden Valley, but to break the awkward silence that had descended over us, partially due to my nervousness at accepting a ride from a stranger, I asked Dane why his grandfather was in the nursing center.

"He had a stroke and went there for rehabilitation."

"Oh, I'm sorry to hear that. "I wanted to ask if his doctor expected a full recovery, but decided it was probably none of my business.

"Yes, but it's just temporary. Gramps hopes to go back home soon."

Darn. I'd hoped I might run into Dane now and then—or more often—since he was there every day. It would be nice to at least know *someone* at my new job. But then, I told myself I shouldn't wish a long stay in rehab on anyone. And if the grandfather was as nice as his grandson, well—

"We're here." Dane's announcement broke into my thoughts.

"Thank you *so* much for rescuing me. You even got me here just in time."

He nodded. "Be sure to call for a tow truck right away," he reminded me. "You might have a long wait for one, judging by the accidents we saw out there."

Oh no, I forgot all about calling. I'm sure he thought I was ditzy. "I will. Thanks for the reminder."

"Well, good luck on your first day, then."

I could tell he was in a hurry, so I didn't linger. "Thanks again." I shut the passenger door of his car with a little wave, turned and walked toward the front entrance of the main building. I heard a light honk of a car horn and looked up to see him wave as he passed by, probably in search of a place to park. I waved again and smiled.

I opened the door and walked through the lobby to the reception area. The woman with graying hair behind the desk, stood when I gave her my name and told her I was the new Marketing Coordinator. She was very tall and big-boned, and her voice was loud and intimidating. She eyed me up and down as we waited for the call to go through and when it did, she announced in her loud voice to the person who answered, "She's here." But then she cupped her hand over the mouthpiece of her headset and as she turned slightly away from me, spoke too quietly for me to hear the rest of the conversation. I felt my face grow warm.

What was she saying about me?

"I'll take you to see Mrs. Braxton, now," the receptionist said, looking down her long nose at me. She pulled the headset wire out of wherever it was attached and walked out from behind the desk. "Follow me," she commanded and set off at a brisk pace.

So I did, down a long hallway to the glass-fronted office at the very end.

CHAPTER TWO

When I got up the next morning and peeked out the window at all the snow still on the ground, I knew I'd made the right decision not to take the rental car my insurance company offered. For one thing, I couldn't have gotten it in the driveway. But even more, after landing my car in a ditch, I didn't feel comfortable driving again until the snow evaporated. This time, I'd walk to work.

There wasn't much of a shoulder on the road. Why hadn't I ever noticed that before? I'd been up and down that road many times. Of course, I'd never walked there, only driven. When I heard a car coming up behind me, I turned around to look, hoping it would give me a wide berth. It didn't. So I stepped away as far as possible, but the car slowed and stopped right next to me. The passenger window slid down.

"Need a ride?" a familiar male voice called.

"Dane?"

"Remember, I told you I visit Gramps every day before work."

Why did he always see me at my worst? My next thought was, *Why did it matter?* I'd just met the man the day before. Still, it was like dashing off to the store in ratty old comfy clothes when you forgot a major ingredient to make a meal and running into someone you knew there. And there I was again, just like yesterday, wearing jeans, rubber boots, mittens, a fuzzy hat and my coat with a hood.

"Come on, Micah, hop in. It's freezing out there," Dane urged me.

"Okay, thanks." I gave in, of course. I wasn't a fool—warm car versus slippery, cold, long walk...with a good-looking man?

"How did your first day on the job go?" Dane glanced at me briefly but mainly kept his eyes on the road, I was glad to see. *Walking* in the frozen ruts had been hard enough, I don't know how he drove in them."Or should I ask about your car first? I didn't see it on my way home last night."

"Oh, yeah. First of all, the receptionist claimed I was supposed to be there at eight o'clock, not eight-thirty. And then, my boss didn't look too happy when I told her I needed to call a tow truck. She said I might as well just go home and make today my official start day instead. And here I am."

"So, I guess you didn't get a rental."

"No. Maybe later. I didn't want to take the

chance of wrecking another car," I said and laughed hollowly. "It sounds like we are supposed to have this cold weather for awhile and maybe even more snow, according to the weather people."

"You should get a car like this," Dane told me. "It's an all-wheel drive Subaru, and great in the snow. I got it 'cause I go up to the mountains a lot for skiing, and for days like this."

"Maybe I will next time...after I've been on the job for awhile, "I replied politely .I'd been out of work too long and glad to have a paid-for car. If my new job didn't work out, I certainly wouldn't have the money for car payments. I just hoped my car wasn't totaled.

"When will you get your car back?" Dane asked.

"I don't know. The auto body shops are really busy right now. When I told the tow truck driver where my insurance company wanted the car to go, he said he'd already taken a couple other cars there that morning. Both the shop and my insurance company told me they wouldn't be able to give me an estimate on the damage right away."

"I'd be happy to drive you to work until you get

a rental. After all, I know where you work, and I'm going there anyway." He smiled.

"I don't want to cause problems for you," I said.

"Why would that cause problems for me?" He turned and gave me a puzzled look.

"I mean, make you late for work."

"Not a problem."

"Okay—until I get a rental, of course."

"Of course." He grinned.

Inside the Golden Valley lobby, I was happy to see that the receptionist wasn't anywhere in sight. I headed to the restroom to change my clothes. It was occupied. I slumped against the wall across from the door. I didn't dare be late after my boss had given me another chance for a first day.

The bathroom door opened abruptly.

"Oh, it's *you*," the receptionist said before she stepped out and walked down the hall.

I felt a headache coming on.

The day never got much better. Between the receptionist—whose name, she informed me was Olga

Hogan—with her snooty attitude, and the amount of information I needed to learn to do my job, when it was finally time to go home, I had a raging headache.

I couldn't figure Olga. What had I done? She seemed pleasant enough to the residents and, as far as I could tell, the other employees. Just my luck, my boss assigned Olga to be my mentor or something. My predecessor, Olga told me, had worked there longer than any of the current employees, and now that she was gone, Olga held that distinction. Could be she resented the extra work—and me.

When I'd originally applied for the marketing coordinator position, there wasn't an actual human resources department at Golden Valley. Lee Jones, the executive director was the one who called me and set up the interview. When we met on Monday, I learned that the woman I'd be replacing, had already retired. Lee didn't seem to know much about what the marketing coordinator job entailed other than "keeping the apartments full." I'd be taking phone calls, answering questions, meeting with prospects, showing apartments, taking down payments, and keeping up the waiting list.

To me, it sounded more like a glorified apartment manager than a marketing position, but he said changes were in the works, including expanding the marketing department and adding a marketing director—potential for growth and an assistant for me.

Lee called back on Friday. He said he was impressed with my experience, and offered me the job.

I'd had a couple phone interviews and another one in person with other companies, but I had no way of knowing what would come of them. I might not get another offer. I accepted.

My cell phone rang early the next day as I was eating breakfast and the screen showed the call was from Golden Valley. Maybe Lee wanted me to come in earlier than the 8:30 a.m. time he'd given me. To my surprise, it wasn't Lee Jones calling. It was Bob Peterson, the new Human Resources Manager, he told me. He wanted me to come to his office on Monday and fill out paperwork after I met with Mrs. Braxton—the *new* executive director and CEO. *What?* Lee said there were changes coming, but he didn't say anything about him leaving.

Mrs. Braxton seemed okay, though I couldn't help wonder how she felt about me. After all, Lee hired me, she didn't. But then, he'd hired most of the staff I guessed—except for Bob who, I learned, she'd brought with her from her previous location, somewhere out of state.

I knew that often when new owners or managers took over a company, they brought in their own people and let the current staff go. Since the board of directors let Lee go, were we all in danger of losing our jobs? One of the other companies I'd interviewed with called me in for a second interview, but I told them "thanks but no thanks." I'd already accepted a job. Maybe I shouldn't have burned my bridges.

When I passed through the lobby just before quitting time, I saw Dane's car parked at the curb in front of the building and sighed in relief. I dashed back to my office, grabbed my boots and jeans and hurried to the restroom to change again.

As I headed for the front door, Olga was still at the reception desk, talking to one of the residents I'd met earlier. "Don't forget to study those materials I gave you today," Olga called out to me.

I nodded. When it looked as though she might say more, I said, "There's my ride. See ya tomorrow," and rushed out the doors.

Dane was all smiles as he held open the passenger-side car door for me. "Well, how was your first real day on the job?" he asked with a grin.

I was too tired to talk, but since he was kind enough to give me a ride, I searched my mind for an appropriate answer. "The staff is friendly," I said at last. And except for Olga, they were. "In fact, they might be the nicest group of people I've ever worked with. We have quite the melting pot. Our employee's manual"—which Olga insisted I read cover to cover the first hour after I arrived—"said the staff is comprised of about eleven different countries, and so far I've met people from Chile, Eritrea, Ethiopia, Mexico, China, India, and Vietnam. I love to hear all the different accents."

"Yeah, I know what you mean. Gramps really likes one of the LPNs. She's very gentle when caring for him. She said at home in the country where she was born, the elderly never go to places like Golden Valley, the families care for them."

I didn't say anything further, and we lapsed into a companionable silence the rest of the way until we got to the bottom of the hill on my street. I saw cars there still covered in snow. I asked Dane to stop, I'd walk home from there. When it looked as though he might resist, I said, "I think a walk in the fresh air would help me get rid of this headache. I always get one the first day of a new job," I assured him when I saw the concerned look on his face.

"Okay, then. Hope you feel better. See you tomorrow morning," Dane said and after I got out of the car, drove off.

CHAPTER THREE

The next morning, she pounced on me as soon as I walked through the automatic double glass doors into the lobby.

"Mrs. Braxton wants to speak to you," Olga told me with a smirk.

"Okay. Do you know why?" She didn't answer, so I asked, "Do I have time to change first?" Though I got a ride most of the way with Dane, I still had to walk down the hill and back up it again in the evening. I wore my jeans, boots, and a heavy coat to work and carried my work pants and shoes to change into when I got there.

"Yes, but be quick. She told me to have you go to her office as soon as you got in this morning."

I walked into my office and dropped my backpack on the floor next to the desk, then changed as fast as I possibly could in the restroom. I hurried back to the office and threw my wet boots into the room, closed the door and headed to the executive director's office.

The door was closed. I knocked and when I heard her say, "Come in," I entered, closing it behind me again. "Have a seat," she said without looking up, just continued to write on a large yellow pad of paper.

I sat there and worried. What could this possibly be about? Was she going to fire me already? I felt yesterday's headache coming back.

Finally, Mrs. Braxton put her pen down and looked up at me.

"How are you this morning, Micah?" Before I could answer, she continued. "Feel like you're getting a handle on the job?"

In just one day? Oh sure, I thought. "I'm getting there," I said instead.

"Good." She smiled at me and then looked at her watch. "I'm sure you have things to do to get ready for the day, and I have a meeting to go to." She stood up, so I did too.

Whew. Was that all the meeting was about? I felt the headache recede a bit as I turned to walk out of the office. But just as I reached the door, Mrs. Braxton spoke again.

"By the way...have you had a chance to read the employee's manual?"

Huh? "Yes."

"Then I'm sure you are aware this organization has a 'non-fraternization policy,' that includes residents and their families."

Had she seen me getting in and out of Dane's car? Or had Olga? If so, I wouldn't put it past her to "tattle" on me to the boss.

I gulped, audibly, I'm sure ."No, ma'am. I guess I missed that."

"Yes, well we do. And now that you know, I'm sure you realize how awkward it would be for us if interactions with our residents' family members became romantic, such as between one of our staff and say...a grandson? Relationships sometimes turn sour, and we could lose the staff member if they become too uncomfortable having that person around and decide to leave us. And just as worrisome, there could be the perception by others here that the resident was given preferential treatment or generally benefitted somehow from the relationship. We certainly can't have that, can we?"

I wanted to say, *What about temporary residents who are only here for a short stay?* But I figured I'd better just leave well enough alone. "No, ma'am."

"Well, I'm glad you understand. Have a good day," she said with a wave of her hand which told me I'd been dismissed—for now.

I walked back to my office deep in thought. What to do? It was still too icy for me to feel comfortable driving. The weather continued to remain cold enough that the snow hadn't melted much and even if it did, it got so cold when the temperature went down at night, the roads just froze up again. I couldn't afford a taxi and I'd heard on the news the night before, that the buses were on emergency schedules and not doing all their regular routes. I wasn't a bus rider and anyway I couldn't remember if I'd ever seen them that far out in the country where I lived.

I *had* to keep riding with Dane—or walk.

When Olga called me an hour later to come out to the reception desk and get my next reading assignment, I told myself to remain calm. I had no proof that she was the one who ratted me out—although, at the time, I didn't know I was doing anything wrong. Fortunately, she was too busy with a group of residents and phone calls to do more than hand me some paperwork and remind me of the managers' meeting at eleven o'clock. Because there wasn't a manager for the marketing department, I would attend the weekly meetings. Olga would not. She was actually part of the business department. I looked forward to meeting the department heads and learning more about the organization, but mostly hoping to find some allies there.

Mrs. Braxton introduced me to the others first thing and though everyone was nice and told me a little bit about what they did at Golden Valley, a couple of the managers really stood out in my mind as people I'd like to get to know. After the meeting, the executive director encouraged me to meet with the various directors and managers. Terri, the activities director, must have overheard and invited me to her office.

When we were seated, Terri looked at me and asked, "So, how are you doing with Olga?" I tried not to react while I thought of the politically correct thing to say, but either because I hesitated or maybe she'd caught the grimace I thought I'd hidden, she continued before I answered. "I was kinda surprised Mrs. Braxton—Lila—pawned her off on you." Terris eyes twinkled and then she grinned.

"I think it's the other way around," I said and laughed.

"Maybe. She likes the power, I think. And I suppose there wasn't anyone else to show you the ropes since Bev already left."

"I wondered about that. Why didn't Golden Valley hire her replacement while she was still here to train them?" I asked. "I assume she gave at least two weeks' notice." I felt relieved to find someone who would answer my questions since Olga wouldn't.

"Well, that was Lee's fault. He just kept putting it off. He was pretty good at procrastinating. "She frowned ."He was a decent guy and okay to work for. Just not motivated, I guess. He was here for fifteen years, and I think he liked things the way they were. That's probably why he lost his job. The board of directors gave him several years to grow this place— "Terri must have seen my bewildered look, for she stopped and explained .

"All the older retirement communities like this are expanding to keep up with the new one's opening. Elder care is a big business now with all the boomers getting older."

"Sad, in a way," I said before I thought about it. After all, it provided *me* with a job when I desperately needed one.

"Yeah," Terri agreed with a sigh. We sat there for

a moment lost in thought."Job security, though," Terri said.

I nodded. "So, who showed the vacant apartments and gave tours of the facility after Bev left? " I asked ."Come to think of it, I don't even know who does it now. I'm supposed to start taking the calls today."

"Marketing, there's a call for you on line one. Marketing, line one, "Olga's voice came over the intercom.

"In fact, there's my first one now. Thanks for the chat." I stood up to leave.

"Good luck," Terri said, as I walked out the door.

I was nervous about answering the call, but it turned out to be fairly easy. The caller, who was looking for housing for her mother, just wanted prices on our various apartments and their availability. I read off the monthly costs from the price sheets Olga had given me and then offered to send out a packet of information to the woman.

Throughout the day, several of the other managers came to my office and chatted. Some just seemed curious about me and others were all business and explained in more detail than they'd given in the meeting, about what they did. One thing they all asked me: where did you work before you came here? And to a person, each one expressed surprise that I'd never worked in the business before. They must have wondered how I got the job—*I* wondered how I got the job. In fact, I'd been kinda surprised I got it with no experience. Many companies I'd interviewed with said that was the reason they didn't hire me—no experience in their field. Finally, the last employee I met with at the end of the day, answered that question.

The nursing director, Val, invited me into her office. She was very friendly and made me feel at ease. Maybe it was her kind face. And it turned out her niece and I had gone to high school together. When she told me she'd been working at Golden Valley for fifteen years, I said, "Oh, you must have started about the same time as Lee."

"Yes, we worked together in another facility up north. They were going through some big not-so-good changes, and we both decided to get out. When Lee got hired on, he recommended me. "She smiled.

"Did you have any idea he was going to be let go?" I asked curiously, and then wished I'd kept my big mouth shut.

But Val didn't seem to mind. "Yeah. I think all of us did—except maybe Lee. The board let him slide for so long, I doubt he thought they'd ever let him go." She sighed. "But it's not the good old boy network here anymore. We've had a lot of turnover on the board lately, and the new ones are younger people, since so many of the others who were here for years, retired.

"Well when I interviewed with him, Lee told me there were big changes in the works. He said he liked my experience, even though I hadn't worked in this business before."

"Yeah, I heard that." She smiled again. "Lee told me," she continued.

"Oh. He discussed the applicants with you, I guess."

"Well, I kept bugging him to hire someone. The other managers were complaining. They thought he wasn't doing anything about it. And then Olga started bugging him too 'cause she wanted the job—"

Val continued to talk, but I tuned her out as soon as I heard the words, *Olga wanted the job.* That's why she was so resentful and spiteful toward me. "Excuse me, Val. I'm sorry, I didn't hear your last few words. You just reminded me of something. Could you say that last part again?"

She thought for a moment. "Oh, I just said that Lee really wasn't putting off hiring someone, he just didn't get many applications and Olga wasn't qualified for the job. She doesn't have any marketing experience. And then you came along and...oh...uh." She stopped talking abruptly. "Well, I'm sure you'll do just fine." She patted my hand and stood up. "Great talking to you, but I have a meeting now, and you probably want to wind things down and go home."

As I walked back to my office, I thought, *Great, I got hired for this job because I was the last resort.*

No time to dwell on that. I needed to change and get outside before Dane showed up at the curb.

CHAPTER FOUR

The next morning as we drove into work, Dane asked, "Have you met Gramps yet?"

"Well no..." I'd purposely stayed away from the nursing care area of Golden Valley as much as possible. I was paranoid about getting caught 'fraternizing with the enemy,' if I got anywhere near Dane or his grandfather or any of their other family members, and losing my job—a job I desperately needed. "I haven't given any tours of the building yet."

"I told Gramps about you on your first day. He'd like to meet you."

"Really?

"Yes. Hey, I know. Why don't you come with me to see him this morning? Just a quick visit before you have to start work."

"You mean now? Today? "I asked in a panic.

He looked at me kinda' funny. "Yes, today, this morning—unless you don't want to, of course." I thought he sounded disappointed when he said it.

Oh no. How could I get out of it without hurting his feelings? After all, he hadn't asked me for anything else and gave me rides to and from work every day. He'd even turned down money for gas, saying he was going my way anyway. I could try to put it off for another day, maybe see if we could come in earlier when there were fewer people around to notice me, but the nurses were there 24/7. *Someone* could recognize me. Or I could wait and hope that his grandfather got well soon so it wouldn't be an issue. No, I couldn't do that. I would run out of excuses.

"Okay," I said. I'd figure something out.

A block before we reached the retirement community, I spoke up. "Dane, can you just pull over to the curb and let me out here?" I searched my brain for a logical reason why. Then I spied a coffee shop. "I need to get coffee first. There won't be time later." I wasn't really a coffee drinker, but maybe they'd have hot chocolate.

He gave me a quizzical look this time. "Uh, sure." He pulled the car up to the curb.

I gathered up my backpack and then looked over

at him before I opened the passenger side door to get out. "I'll meet you there in a few. What room is your grandfather in?"

No time to stand in line for my supposed coffee or hot chocolate, so I looked around to see if Dane had really driven off. When I didn't see him, I hurried to Golden Valley, changed my clothes, dumped everything in my office and shut the door. I dashed through the lobby and out the door into the residents' parking lot and then walked quickly around the building. This time, I went through the back door entrance. I knew there were cameras at the reception desk that monitored all the outside doors, but since Olga wasn't at the desk, I hoped if she saw me, she would think I just got there.

As I walked through the doors to the nursing center, and then down the hallway, peering into the rooms as I passed, a couple nurses smiled and said, "Morning." Maybe they thought I was a visitor. I didn't think I'd worked there long enough for them to know me, and I wasn't wearing my nametag. Hopefully, I could squeak by. Surely, Dane wouldn't ask me again.

Finally, at the last room on the left side of the

hallway, I heard Dane's deep voice. "She'll be here any minute, Gramps." She won't be able to stay long, though, she has to work."

I peered inside the open door and saw Dane seated in a chair by a hospital bed. An older, white-haired man lay in the bed, under a sheet and colorful afghan. I pasted a smile on my face and rapped my knuckles on the open door. "Hi, it's me, Micah. May I come in?"

"Here she is now, Gramps. Come in, Micah, come in," Dane said cheerfully and then looked around the room as I walked in and stood next to him. "The other chair is missing. Here, take mine and I'll look for another one." He started to rise, but I put my hand on his shoulder.

"Don't get up. I can't stay for long. I have to get to work." I looked over at his grandfather and smiled. Nice to meet you, Mr.—" I paused, realizing I didn't know his last name. I didn't know if he was Dane's grandfather on his mom's side or his dad's.

"Crawl," his grandpa said in a guttural voice.

Umm. I looked at Dane.

"Carl," Dane told me. He smiled at his

grandfather. "It's a little hard for him to talk right now...since his stroke. But he's getting better all the time. Pretty soon you'll be telling jokes again, right Gramps?"

I looked from Dane back to his grandfather. I wasn't used to calling people my grandparents' age by their first name. "You want me to call you Carl?" I asked him.

"Ess." He nodded.

I heard voices out in the corridor and realized the nurses' shift was probably changing and there would be more of a chance that the day shift staff might know me.

"Well...*Carl*...I'm so glad I got to meet you. I hope you are getting wonderful care here. I have to get back downstairs to work now. You take care," I said in a rush. I put a hand on Dane's shoulder. "See you later," I told him, as I walked swiftly to the doorway and peered out into the hallway.

I slipped out to the sound of Dane's voice, "Later."

And then another, slower voice, "Sheeze purrdee."

I smiled all the way back down the hallway until

I saw my antagonist, Olga, standing in front of the reception desk. I sighed. As I crossed the wide, carpeted lobby, I saw her eyes dart to the large clock on the wall then back at me with a frown. She was probably annoyed that I was there early. But to my surprise, she said, "You're late."

I looked down at my watch which I hadn't worn in a long time—I usually relied on my smartphone—but began wearing again since I started the job. It was easier than digging my phone out of my pocket every time I got asked for the time—which happened a lot during my walks through the complex. My watch showed I was *exactly* on time. I looked to see Olga smirking at me. I decided to ignore her.

"You must have got your car back," she surprised me by saying.

"What?" I looked at her, puzzled about her remark.

"You're not wearing your 'walking' clothes." She gestured.

Uh-oh. I hadn't thought about that. My life was getting more and more complicated. I hated lying. If I didn't need the job so bad, I wouldn't be in this predicament. I could tell Olga to just take the job and shove—

"Morning, Olga, Micah," Terri said as she walked past us. She stopped part way down the hall to her office. "Say, Micah...can you stop by when you're done there?"

"Sure. I—" I heard the phone ring and then another, and Olga stepped back behind the desk and plugged in. And when it kept on ringing, she waved me away. When I just stood there, she covered the mouthpiece of her headset.

"Just go," she said irritably and sat down.

Saved by the bell, I thought. But when I looked at Terri, I saw her wink.

I followed her down the hall to her office. "What did you want to talk about?" I asked her as she walked in and sat down.

"Nothing, really. You just looked like you didn't want to answer her question, so I made it up to get you away from Olga." She grinned.

"Thanks, Terri. I owe you one."

"Anytime," she said.

The rest of my first week passed by quickly and by Friday, the sun came out, the snow was actually melting, and there were bare patches on the roads, including the hill to my house. And that afternoon, the auto body shop called me with the estimate on my car. I was left gasping at the cost but at least it was fixable, and my insurance would pay most of it. I'd have to put the deductible on my credit card and make payments.

I called my insurance company and told the woman there that I was ready to get a rental car. Would this afternoon be too soon? Maybe Dane could drop me off. And after that, I would find some way to avoid him

"You *are* aware that you don't have car rental on your insurance policy, aren't you ma'am?"

"*What?* " I gasped again. "But...but I'm sure I—"

"Actually, let's see...it shows here you spoke with your agent...and discontinued that part of your policy on June first of this year."

Oh. Oh no. That's right. When a few months passed and I still didn't have a job, I'd looked for ways to cut costs. I'd taken the chance I wouldn't need the rental car part of my insurance policy and asked him to take it off to lower my monthly payments.

"Okay, well thanks," I said, ready to hang up.

"Would you like to add it back onto your policy?"

"Will I be able to get a rental car then? "I asked hopefully.

"No, sorry. Not for this incident, but next time you need one."

"Uh, not yet. Thanks." I hung up. I couldn't believe my luck.

Every day that week I'd ridden to work and back with Dane, I'd told myself that as soon as the snow melted enough, I'd get the rental car. Sure, I'd miss riding with him—I'd been surprised to learn how much we had in common, and he was "easy on the eyes" as my grandmother used to say—but I wouldn't miss the clench in my gut every time I got in or out of his car at work. I was so worried someone—particularly Olga who wanted my job—would report me to Mrs. Braxton. Now I definitely couldn't afford to lose it.

I needed to let Dane know the situation, that I wouldn't be getting a rental car and that it would probably be a month before I got my car back. The auto body shop was backed up with cars from accidents during the snowstorm. At least he hadn't asked me to visit his grandfather—Carl—again.

About an hour before quitting time, Dane called. We'd finally exchanged phone numbers in case one of us couldn't meet on time for some reason. "Hey," he said.

"What's up?" I asked. "Gotta work late...on a Friday? That sucks."

"No, but I have to do something for Gramps. I could run you home first, but I thought you might like to go with me."

"Sure, if that's more convenient for you."

"Doesn't matter about that. I just thought you might like to go with me to check on Gramps's horse."

Horse? "Did you say your grandfather's 'horse'?"

I'd always wanted a horse, from as far back as I could remember. When I was younger, I'd asked for a pony every year on my birthday and then again for

Christmas. From the age of ten years old on, I'd asked for a horse.

My mother just said, "I wanted a horse too when I was a girl. You grandfather told me, 'If wishes were horses, then beggars would ride.' I never got a horse. You'll get over it like I did. Soon, you'll be a teenager and meet some boy and forget all about horses."

My grandfather said to me, "We had horses when I was growing up. 'Course ours were work horses on the farm. You live in the city. Where would you keep it?"

Maybe it was just as well. My parents split up. Mom and I moved into an apartment, and there was never any extra money. Even though I earned money through babysitting for several families in our huge complex, it wasn't enough to buy and keep a horse.

But I never stopped wanting one.

CHAPTER FIVE

When I got in the car, I noticed Dane wore work boots. He'd told me to be sure and wear the rubber boots I'd worn to work every day that week.

"Where does your—Carl—keep his horse? At home?"

"No, when Gram died, he sold their house and moved into a condo. He boards Misty about a mile up the street from there."

"Have you ever ridden her?"

"Me? No, I don't know much about horses. I guess Gramps and his brother had them when they were teenagers, but had to sell them when they went off to serve in the military during World War II. When he got out, he met Gram, and they moved to the city. I guess Gram had fallen off a horse and never wanted to ride again, so he didn't get another horse for a long time. When she died, he said Misty helped him to have a purpose in life. He spent a lot of time with her, sometimes just grooming or talking to her while she ate."

"I'll bet he misses her. How long since he's seen her?

"Oh...a couple months, I guess."

When we pulled into a gravel driveway, I noticed long grass poking through the remainder of the snow. Snow weighed heavily on the barbed wire fences that surrounded the pastures. Horses stood outside eating hay on the ground, scattered in brackish puddles of water and snow. I looked down from the high seats of Dane's SUV and saw the water in the trough appeared to be frozen solid. Were the horses expected to depend on the snow and puddles on the ground for water? The roof of one lean-to had collapsed under the weight of the snow as well and almost touched the ground. The horses looked wet and cold. Why didn't they wear blankets?

"Has anyone in your family been out here to check on Misty lately?" I asked, appalled by the condition of the place.

"I don't know for sure. I thought my aunt was going to. I would have come sooner if I hadn't been so busy with this big project at work."

And taking me to and from work, I thought. He

hadn't once been late. Now I wondered if he was going back to work after he dropped me off in the evenings. He hadn't yet told me what he did for a living and I hadn't asked, assuming that when I quit getting a ride with him, I probably wouldn't see him. But this wasn't the time or place.

"Hmm."

Dane parked the Subaru, and we got out. I headed for the barn. Right away, I caught the smell of old, moldy hay. I glanced into the first stall I came to and saw what appeared to be dried up horse manure and dirty shavings. Each stall I passed was in the same condition. They didn't look as though they had been cleaned in a long, long time. At least there were no horses in them. When I walked out the other end of the barn, I saw some paddocks. There, the horses stood in mud over their ankles, and just like the horses in the pasture, ate hay off the ground.

"Gramps doesn't keep Misty in the barn. She should be in one of the pastures with a walk-in shelter," Dane said in a subdued tone. He hadn't said a word until then. Even though he wasn't a horse person, I'm sure he could see how bad the conditions were. If not, he saw the scowl on my face. Then he pointed to a horse. "There she is."

We slogged our way over. I could see why he'd told me to wear my boots. I don't know if the snow melting caused all the mud, but I hoped so. Although I'd just met him once, I couldn't believe Carl would keep his horse in a place like this all the time. The horse Dane lead me to was brown and white, although the "white" parts of her were brownish, blackish, green. Just like the others, she was eating hay in the mud. It looked as though she hadn't been groomed in ages. Her long mane lay in matted clumps, and her long, whitish, ragged tail hung to the ground. It was missing large clumps where I figured she must be stepping on it. Her hooves, what I could see of them in the deep mud, were overgrown. She stopped eating and stared at us.

"Hey, Misty," I said softly. Her ears perked when I said her name. "I'm sorry, girl. I don't have a treat for you."

"That's right. Gramps usually shares an apple with her."

"Next time, then, Misty," I said. What was I saying? I didn't know if there would be a next time. The walk-in stall was just as bad as all the others. It looked as though it hadn't been cleaned in a long time. There wasn't a single dry spot for a horse to stand, much less lie down.

We didn't see anyone around the whole time we were there, nor any cars or trucks parked in the driveway. We walked back to the Subaru in silence. But as we drove back down the gravel road, I couldn't keep quiet any longer.

"What are you going to do? The conditions in that place are deplorable!"

"Yeah, it didn't look good to me either, but are you sure it isn't just because it's winter and the snow and all?" Dane turned toward me.

"It's *definitely* more than that. You have to get Misty out of there. And then call the sheriff and tell them what is—or actually, isn't—going on there."

"Yeah, I guess you're right. I don't know anything about the place, or the people who own it. I've been there a couple times with Gramps, but I don't remember it looking like that. It was in the summer, though."

"I don't know about that, but it's bad now. I think your grandfather would be horrified. Are you going to tell him?"

"I'll have to. Then I can ask him where he wants to move Misty. I don't know of any boarding facilities, do you?"

"No, but we could look on the Internet or ask for recommendations from feed stores or vets in this area. I'd be happy to do it. I could make the calls on my lunch break."

"Would you? That's great." Dane looked relieved.

I'd have to get prices too. I didn't know what Carl could afford, but I imagined being a senior citizen, he was on a limited budget. Maybe that was why he'd chosen to keep Misty at that place, it was all he could afford. I knew how *that* was.

I was so deep in thought, I didn't realize Dane had driven past the spot where he usually let me off at the bottom of the hill and was headed up to my road. "So, where do you live?" he asked me.

"You can let me off here," I said, gathering up my backpack.

"Micah, it's dark and there aren't any street lights on this road. If I'd known that before, I never would have just dropped you off at the bottom of the hill. So let me take you to your house, okay?"

House? This is what I had tried to avoid all week. I sighed. "Okay, next driveway on the right." When he pulled up to the place I rented, I could imagine what he must think. There was a real stigma to my type of home—especially the metal-sided kind. But it was all I could afford.

"You have a barn on your property? Cool," Dane enthused. He got out of the Subaru and headed toward the faded red barn, pulling a flashlight out of his coat pocket as he crunched through the slushy snow which had already refrozen in the cold night air.

"Yes, it came with the property. It used to be a farm, but the owners sold off the rest of the property bit by bit. This is all that's left." I waved my hand to encompass the manufactured home and barn that sat on almost two and a half acres.

"You could keep Misty here."

"Oh, I don't know..."

"There's plenty of room and you have a barn."

"But I don't own this place, I rent it. I don't know if I could keep a horse here. And even if I could, look at the fences. Except for the one side between this place and the neighbors, they're falling down, with rusty barbed wire and rotting posts. And the barn is old..." By then we'd reached the barn. With one hand, Dane grabbed the thick wooden handle on one of the heavy wooden doors and attempted to open it. Then he used both hands and yanked on it. Because it hung askew, it dragged across the grass and dirt, and finally opened.

Inside, it was dirty and smelled musty, with huge cobwebs draped across the entrance and most of the interior. The stanchions for milking cows could still be seen, but obviously hadn't been used in years. I looked up when I saw light coming through the a hole in the ceiling which was the floor of the hay loft above, I suspected the floor underneath must be wet. I pointed it out to Dane.

"Yeah, but most of the barn is dry. It would be easy to patch the roof and with a few boards, I could make a nice stall." Dane seemed to be talking to himself.

"What about the fences?"

"No problem. We could put in some metal posts and hang some wire and with a controller, we'd have an electric fence. The monthly board Gramps will pay you for Misty should more than cover the cost of extra water and electricity."

We? That would mean me spending more time with Dane, which in ordinary circumstances, I wouldn't mind at all. In fact—No, I couldn't think that way. I needed to keep my job. I needed the money to fix my car. I'd forgotten the credit card was another thing I canceled. It was too tempting when I wasn't working. If I couldn't afford it, I didn't buy it.

"In fact, let me write you a check for the first month right now,» Dane said and pulled a checkbook out of his inside coat pocket."

"No. I can't accept that. I don't even know if the landlord will let me keep a horse here," I protested weakly. Maybe I would get lucky and the owner would say no.

"Can you call right now? Either way, take the check. You can always give it back to me."

Man, there was just no way to discourage the guy.

CHAPTER SIX

Dane asked if he could come inside while I made the call, and I reluctantly agreed. It was too cold for him to stay outside. Although he could sit in his car with the engine running and the heater on, that would be rude. I was just so embarrassed for him to see inside the "tin can" I lived in. With the metal siding, it was cold in the winter and hot in the summer. At least I was just renting. And yet, I liked that I no longer lived in an apartment as I had all of my adult life and teen years. And it was fun to decorate when I could pound all the holes in the walls I wanted.

I flipped on the inside light and waited for Dane to either say something or be too polite to say a word.

"Hey, this is nice. It feels...cozy," he said and smiled. "Mind if I look around while you call your landlord?" he asked as he looked at the framed pictures on the entertainment center, mostly of my mom and me.

"Uh, sure, if you want to."

As I waited for the call to the owner to go

through, the longer it took for him to answer, the more hopeful I felt. But just as I'd decided to hang up, he answered the phone, sounding out of breath. And when I told him what I wanted to do, he said, "Sure, go for it. Do anything you want. It probably won't hurt anything and might help the value of the real estate. But it's your dime, I'm not paying for anything. And don't be surprised if your utilities bills go up.»

I assured him I was aware of all that, and then we hung up.

"What did he say?" Dane asked eagerly.

I could lie and tell him the landlord said no, but I wouldn't. We *had* to get Misty out of that terrible place. So I told him. "He said it was okay."

"Whoo-hoo!" Dane shot a fist into the air. "That's terrific." He pulled a small notebook out of his shirt pocket and began to write on it, muttering to himself as he did. Then he stopped abruptly and looked up. "Are you hungry?"

He must have heard my stomach rumble.

"Well, yeah. But my fridge is about bare. I was going to ask you to drop me off at the mini-mart, but I guess I got a little distracted."

"I'm sorry. That was my fault. We could go somewhere and grab something to eat, or we could have pizza delivered here. I want to get this list of supplies made out—with your help, of course—and then pick up everything we need in the morning at the hardware store and maybe the feed store. I'm sure I have enough lumber lying around to do the job…oh—"he reached around and pulled his wallet from his jean pocket—"I could eat a whole pizza just by myself. So order two large—pepperoni, sausage and Canadian bacon for me and whatever you want—and a liter bottle of something to drink, okay?"

"I'm sorry, I don't have any beer in my fridge." Most guys our age liked beer, but I didn't and didn't keep it around anymore for those who did. No one ever visited me since I'd moved here, so far from Seattle."

He pulled out three twenty dollar bills and handed them to me. "That's okay. I have to drive home anyway. Oh, and here's the check for Misty's board. Is five hundred dollars enough?"

Five Hundred! I could pay my deductible on my

auto insurance. "It's...it's...fine," I answered in a whisper.

"Okay, good. I can pick you up first thing in the morning and drop you off at the store to do your grocery shopping while I get the supplies, if you want."

I barely had time to nod, before he looked back at his notepad.

"Let's see, we'll need some two by six tongue and groove lumber...hmm, I might not have that on hand. Four by fours...yeah, got those. We'll need sixteen penny galvanized nails...You said this was a dairy farm? So, the floor should be all concrete. And for the fences, we agreed on electric—for now, anyway. So, a spool of electric fencing wire, insulators, studded T-posts, fencer, handle for the gate...can you think of anything else?" He looked up at me, pushing back a lock of wet hair that had fallen forward over his brow. I'd become fixated on it and had to shake myself out of it to answer him.

"No...well, honestly, I wouldn't know. I've never built a fence. And for someone who doesn't know much about horses, how do you know so much about it?"

"I might not know much about horses, but I've

put up a lot of fences. That reminds me, I'd better look to make sure I still have the wire stretcher and fence tool. Maybe I should get a bag of staples as well, in case we can use some of the old wooden posts. Hmm...I wonder how hard the ground is? Oh, and the post hole digger of course—"

A knock on the door interrupted him. I was glad to see the pizza delivery guy. The smell of the pizzas in their boxes about made me feel faint, I was so hungry. At least he stopped to eat for awhile, I suspected because Dane couldn't hold a slice and write with greasy fingers at the same time. After he'd devoured most of his pizza, he stretched, sighed and then picked up the notebook and pen again, stopping only to ask, "Do you have gloves—leather work gloves?"

"No"—I shook my head—"I haven't had any need for them."

"Okay, we'll have to get you some. I don't think I have any your size. They don't come in small. You could probably wear mediums..."

I wrapped my pizza with plastic wrap and put it in the refrigerator. "Are you going to eat this last piece of yours?" I asked Dane.

"Huh?" He looked up at me. I asked again and he said, "Oh just leave it there," and went back to calculating how many rolls of wire, how many posts and how many insulators we needed for fencing a property this size.

And so it went until I couldn't keep from yawning and eventually Dane heard me. He looked at his watch and then at me, catching me in the midst of another yawn.

"I'd better go home. It's later than I thought, and you look tired." He snatched the last slice of pizza off the table, grabbed up the box, and then looked around the kitchen.

"Here, I'll take that." I stood too and held out my hand for the box. As he handed it to me, our hands brushed and I felt a quick jolt like electricty. I'd been fighting my attraction to him, but for some reason, circumstances kept throwing us together, it seemed. I found it hard to remain aloof. This was the take-charge Dane. It seemed to come natural to him. In fact, so much so, I wondered once again about his job. Whatever his work, he must be a supervisor.

Dane stood by the door with his coat and hat on, when I turned around from the cupboard under the sink where I kept the garbage pail.

"So, I'll pick you up at...seven o'clock tomorrow morning?"

I felt my eyes widen. It had been a long, tiring, stressful week and I'd hoped to sleep in. In order to be ready at seven o'clock, I'd need to get up almost as early as I did during the week.

"Too early? I thought we could go somewhere for breakfast and by the time we're done and I drop you off at the grocery store—the hardware, feed store and maybe lumberyard if I can't find the T&G at the big-box store—should be open."

"Well, I—"

"You don't want to go food shopping on an empty stomach."

"I have foo—"

"I saw inside the refrigerator when you put the rest of your pizza away. I bet that was going to be breakfast, huh?"

Darn. Could he read me already, having known me less than a week?

"Come on, I'm buying."

"You already gave me a check—"

"That was for Misty's board. This is different. You gotta eat. Don't worry, you'll earn it. I'll work you hard." He laughed, opened the door and stepped out onto my tiny porch. "See you at seven o'clock then," he said with a wave of his hand as he walked down the steps.

"Okay. Thanks for dinner, "I called back, then closed the door to shut out the cold, dark night air.

I couldn't believe how complicated my life had become. I was getting more and more deeply involved with Dane and his family. I knew I shouldn't let it happen. I needed to distance myself from them, but what could I do? I just hoped that I could keep my job long enough to put some money aside for my next period of unemployment.

CHAPTER SEVEN

I'd just finished getting dressed a couple minutes before seven o'clock on Saturday morning, when I heard the loud sound of a vehicle with a diesel engine outside. I pushed the bedroom curtain aside and saw a large pickup backing into my driveway. Probably someone turning around. But then, to my surprise, I noticed the words painted on the door: Andersen Construction and Development. The driver shut the loud thing off, opened the cab door and walked around to the back of the truck. It was Dane.

"Sorry I'm late. Took me longer than I thought to round up the lumber from one of our sites, and look, I found some hinges for the hay loft doors."

Late?

"I gotta unload this before I pick up the rest of the supplies." He pulled the tailgate down, and started to pull out some boards.

"Need some help?" I asked.

"Sure. That will make the job go quicker. Oh, here. We had some in your size after all." He reached into his jacket, pulled something out and tossed it to me. "Work gloves."

We made quick work of pulling the boards out and stacking them in a pile, then covering them with a blue tarp. After I'd locked the front door and grabbed my purse, phone and grocery list, I climbed into the warm cab of the truck.

"Was there any place in particular you wanted to eat?" I asked Dane. Before he could answer, I continued, "I know a place. It's kind of a hole-in-the-wall, but the food is great and they give you lots of it." My plan was to go somewhere in the opposite direction from Golden Valley, even farther out in the country, where I hoped no one from work would see us.

Dane said, "Sounds great. Lead me to it."

Another thing, the food was cheap. I felt guilty that he had to pay for my meals. Until I got that first paycheck, money was tight. Maybe someday I could pay him back.

If I hadn't had to tell Dane where to turn and what

roads to take, I might have fallen asleep, it was so warm and cozy in the truck. Country-western music played softly on the radio.

"Hey, turn that up. I love this song," I told him.

"Oh yeah? Me too," he said with a grin and turned the sound up *loud*. Pretty soon, we were both singing along to the music, me stomping my feet on the floorboards and Dane tapping out the beat on the steering wheel. We finished up with a flourish, then looked at each other and laughed.

I think we were both pretty jazzed—I know I was—by the time we pulled into the puddle-filled gravel parking lot in front of what might have once been a farmhouse. I'd discovered it one day when I was out driving around, trying to get to know my new home. I'd felt a bit leery about eating there, considering the faded paint and sagging porch, but the parking lot that day was nearly full, so I figured there was something about the place that brought them in. I'd gone inside to find out why. I just hoped Dane would like it too.

Luckily, he found a place to park his big pickup. Dirt-encrusted farm trucks shared the parking lot with mini-vans, two-seaters and sedans. When he opened the door for me, the sound of voices and laughter and the smells of home-cooking, wafted out.

A waitress walked up with two menus and told us to sit wherever we wanted. I spotted a small table with two chairs, that appeared to be available, though not yet cleared, and pointed it out to Dane. "How about that one?"

He nodded and followed me across the wooden floors. I could feel his warm hand just barely touching my back, as though letting me know he was there. His touch felt good—too good. When we were seated, the waitress handed us the large, laminated menus, asked if we wanted coffee and said she'd be back to take our order in a few, although she returned pretty quickly with a coffee for Dane and hot chocolate with whipped cream on top, for me.

"They have great omelets. For just under five dollars, you can build an omelet from your choice of ingredients. The plate comes mounded high with farm-style potatoes and toast," I babbled nervously, as we looked over the menus. "And for just fifty cents more, you can order biscuits and gravy, and you won't leave hungry." I'm sure I sounded like a commercial on TV, but Dane's touch was still on my mind.

"Man, that sounds good. I'll get the omelet, but if I added the biscuits and gravy, I'd need to take a nap, and we wouldn't get anything done today." He laughed. "But you go ahead."

"Are you kidding? I can't even eat a whole omelet."

The waitress came and took our orders, and then Dane and I looked around the two mid-sized dining areas that pretty much took up the whole place. Every nook and cranny and wall space was filled with a hodgepodge of furniture from different eras that somehow blended, along with plows and other farm implements, harnesses and collars, milk cans, three-legged milking stools, wooden wheels, country-style crafts, old family photos from the turn of the previous century, dolls with porcelain faces, arms and legs, lace doilies, china teacups, glass beer mugs and tattered old books—like a museum. I figured it would take several visits to see everything.

"Cool," I thought Dane said, but I wasn't sure. The drawback to the two open rooms, separated only by a step-down stairway, was all the noise of clattering spoons and forks, glasses and dishes and the voices of many people, including some families with small children.

"What did you say?" I leaned forward across the table. It seemed as though the volume had risen since we'd arrived.

Dane started to speak, but must have thought better of it. He stood, picked up his chair and carried it to my side of the table, then set it down next to me. Even so, it was still hard to carry on a conversation—especially when a young child began to wail—so we ended up with our heads practically together. I felt his warm breath on my face, and I couldn't help staring into his startling deep blue eyes when he looked in mine and said, "Great decor."

"Wait till you taste the food," I managed to reply. And then it arrived at our table, and we concentrated on eating for the next thirty minutes.

Finally, Dane put his fork down and pushed back from the table. "That's more than I eat at Thanksgiving." He groaned and then looked over at my plate. I had stopped eating as well. "Do you want to take the rest of that home? You only ate about half of it."

"Yeah, this would be great warmed up for breakfast tomorrow."

The waitress came back to our table, gathered up the dishes and said she'd be back with my leftovers as well as the bill. The volume of noise had gone down somewhat as the other diners finished their meals and left, so I heard what she said. I thought Dane might move his chair back to the other side of the table, since it was no longer necessary to shout, but he remained where he was next to me. His right leg was very close to my left. I tried to subtly shift my legs away, but I couldn't. One of the table legs blocked me in. So I looked at the walls and tried to keep the nearness of his limbs from my mind.

When the waitress came back, Dane looked at the tab, handed her several bills and told her to keep the change. The he stood, grabbed his coat off the back of his chair and shrugged it on. I stood too but before I could grab my coat, he whisked it off my chair and said, "Here, allow me."

I must've looked totally shocked as he held the coat and helped me into it.

"What? Haven't your other dates done this for you?"

"No," I managed to say, but I was focusing on just the two words I heard in his sentence, 'other dates.' I needed to talk to him. I decided when we got in the truck, that I would use the drive back to tell him why we couldn't date. But if I did, would he be offended and stop giving me rides to work and back? Then I'd have to use the board money for a rental car instead of paying for...Wait, I couldn't even get a rental car without a credit card. So, once again, I decided not to say anything yet.

We walked toward the front door, but as I started to step out, he turned and said, "Wait here for a minute, while the truck warms up. It has a remote start." He held up the key chain in his hand. Sure enough, I looked out the window and saw exhaust pluming out from the tailpipes.

After we'd driven a few miles in silence, I again felt myself being lulled into sleep by the cab's warmth and now a full stomach, I figured I should start talking. There was something I wanted to ask him, but kept slipping my mind. Then I remembered.

"Did you borrow this truck from your father?" I blurted. When he looked surprised, I added, "You always pick me up in the Subaru."

"I think it's one of the older ones we purchased. We lease the rest. But Dad likes to own at least one, and usually buys one when the lease is up. He took over that part of the business when Gramps pretty much retired. But Gramps still comes into the office and bugs Mom—she's our bookkeeper—"

"You know where I work and what I do, but you've never told me what you do for a living."

"Yeah? Well, I guess you never asked." He grinned.

Marilyn Conner Miles

CHAPTER EIGHT

Dane's timing was great. I had just finished my grocery shopping when he pulled up in front of the store and helped me load the bags onto the truck's back seat. The pickup's bed was full of rolls or wire, tools, more lumber, plastic bags of smaller items and some larger things I couldn't see. Dane had also grabbed some sandwiches, chips and sodas for our lunch. "When we get hungry enough to eat again," he said. "I'm still full from breakfast."

"Me too."

"I felt like taking a nap on the drive back," he admitted. "You looked as though you were about to fall asleep too," he added.

"Yeah, but the cold air has revived me." I laughed.

While I put the groceries away, Dane unloaded the truck. He'd driven through the pasture and right up to the barn.

The rest of the day flew by. While Dane used the pickup's tailgate like a tool bench and a couple sawhorses to cut the lumber, I cleaned out the barn the best I could. Dane had picked up a few tools at the feed store—a pitchfork, rake, shovel, push broom, rubber feed dishes, galvanized garbage cans to hold the feed and a large scoop, plus a 100 gallon water trough and even a floating tank heater to keep Misty's water from freezing, he said the clerk had suggested.

"Next time, you'll have to go with me so we can get whatever else we need. I just told the clerk about Misty and Gramps and that I didn't know what he had for her, and what belonged to the people where he boarded. Tomorrow after church, I'll see Gramps and find out what kind of food she needs. The feed store clerk said they were open after one o'clock tomorrow afternoon. I'll bring it here and then we can go get the trailer on the way to pick up Misty."

By the time I got the area of the barn cleaned where Dane planned to build the stall, he had some lumber cut and I got to be a carpenter's helper. I held up one end of a board while he nailed. We didn't talk much since he was either concentrating on what he was doing or his mouth was full of nails gritted in his teeth, so he could use both hands. I didn't mind not talking, it gave me a chance to watch Dane at work.

When he'd driven to and from work every day the past week, he'd worn a heavy winter jacket. It wasn't until the night before, while we ate pizza sitting at my table, that I'd seen him without it. I'd tried not to stare but, even under his woolen shirt, I had seen that he had a well-defined upper torso, which I assumed was from working out at a gym. He must have gotten too warm, sawing, because he'd taken off the outer shirt and was down to a long-sleeved, navy blue Henley. It stretched tightly across his muscled chest and shoulders. Now I knew where those muscles came from—the hard physical labor of construction work. And though he might spend part of his day behind a desk in the office, or riding around in a work truck, driving from site to site, I could tell that much of his time was also spent in physical labor. He knew exactly what needed to be done and how to do it, as he measured, sawed and hammered together a wonderful, roomy stall with a built-in feed trough. He also re-hung the barn door so that it no longer dragged across the ground. And when that was done, we put up the electric fence around the pasture. He said he'd fix the hanging hay loft doors when we had more time.

Dane hadn't wanted to stop and eat our late afternoon lunch, concerned about getting everything done before dark, so I brought the sandwiches and drinks outside. By then, we were so hungry from working, we wolfed the sandwiches down and drank the sodas. Later, I brought out hot chocolate to warm us up.

"Sorry, I don't have coffee," I apologized when I handed him a mug.

"This is good. I haven't had hot chocolate in a long time." He took a swig. "Say, this is good? What did you put in it?"

"It comes this way. Its peppermint cocoa."

Already, the sky had grown darker. I hoped we could get the fence done before the sun set. Without streetlights on my rural road, it was pitch-dark at night, and we'd have to work by flashlight. Dane was happy to find that the reason the single light in the barn didn't work was only because the bulb was burned out and not because of a lack of—or faulty—wiring.

As we walked the fence line, Dane pounding the metal posts into the ground at intervals—which went in surprisingly easy, for the most part—and checking the old wooden posts, I noticed some movement out of the corner of my eye. And then, a long face reached out and bit me. I jumped back and squealed. That, of course, spooked the horse and he hurried away as fast as he could go in the snow, snorting all the way.

Dane dropped the fencing tool and spun around. "What the heck was that?" he roared, grabbing my arm. "Are you okay?"

"Yeah, sorry. That was the neighbor's horse, Caleb."

"Oh. Is he friendly?"

"Yeah...except for occasional nips."

"Huh. So...Misty won't be alone here after all."

"Yes, he *love*s other horses. He just bites people."

"Great," Dane said. And as he reached down and picked up the fencing tool and the wire spool I'd dropped on the ground, I thought I heard him mutter, "I'll definitely stay away from *that* horse."

With frozen faces, toes, and fingers turning numb, Dane and I finished putting up the wire fence. Then Dane installed the electric fencer on a wall in the barn. It was pitch black outside, and the bare bulb inside didn't put out enough light to work by. My porch light didn't do much either, so Dane had switched on his truck's headlights, while I patiently held he flashlight and pointed it where he directed.

"Okay, that should be it. All we have to do is turn it on and—voilà, "Dane said as he flipped the switch. Then we waited.

"How do you know if it's working?" I asked.

He grinned. "Well, you could go out there and touch the wire."

"I don't think so," I scoffed.

"Yeah, you're right." He pulled something out of his pocket and held it up to the light. "There's a tool for that, see?" He frowned. "But this fencer should be making a sound like a loud clock ticking...and I don't hear anything."

I didn't either. I was so tired and cold and hungry, I just wanted to go in the house, warm up a can of soup and plop down on the sofa. "Maybe you could finish this tomorrow in the daylight—you know, when it's not freezing outside," I suggested hopefully.

"No, I gotta get this figured out tonight." He looked up. "But you can go inside if you want. It *is* cold out here, especially standing around."

Maybe he'd like some time alone to concentrate. "I'll stay if you need help, or I can make some more hot chocolate, or tea...or even heat up some soup."

"Sure, that would be great," Dane answered not really paying attention. I left, and wondered if he even realized I'd gone.

Inside, I noticed I'd had a call on my cell phone. It was my neighbor, so I called her back.

"I see you and some good-looking guy out there putting up a fence," she said when she answered the phone.

I decided to ignore the reference to Dane's appearance. "Yeah, I'm going to board a horse for his family. A girl horse."

"A mare? Caleb will like that. I think he's been a bit lonely this year since Justine went off to college and now you're back at work. When's she coming?"

"The plan is to pick her up tomorrow afternoon—if he gets the electric fencer to work."

"Wow. You work fast."

"We're anxious to get her out of the place where she's boarded now. She's not getting good care. In fact, none of the horses there are. Once we get her out, we're going to call the sheriff."

"Have you talked to the horse rescue organization? You say there are several horses? If they need some help hauling them out, I'd be happy to help with our trailer."

"Oh, that's wonderful, Sonya. Do you have the number for the rescue group?"

"Yeah, somewhere. I'll look for it and call you right back, okay?"

"Sure." As I waited for her call, I put a couple mugs of soup in the microwave, and before they were done, Sonya called back with the number. I wrote it down, then confessed, "I have to admit, I'm a little nervous about tomorrow. I've never hauled a horse before, and neither has Dane, I don't imagine. I don't know if we can even get her into the trailer."

"Does he have a horse trailer?"

"No, he plans to rent one."

"Oh, I've seen those. They're often kinda small and not in the best shape. Tell you what, would you like me to come with you? In fact, I would be happy to haul her in my trailer. It's pretty big. It might make her feel less anxious."

"Really? That would be great. Let me check with Dane, though. I'm going back out there, so can I call you back in a bit?"

"Sure, no problem. I'll be here."

I went back out to the barn with the mugs of soup. "How's it going?" I asked as I handed him one. He took it and downed all the contents in one big swig. "Uh, wasn't that a little hot?"

He didn't seem to notice. "Do you hear that?" he asked with a big grin on his face.

I listened. And then I heard it.

Clunk...clunk...clunk.

"It's working?"

"Yup. "And before I could congratulate him, Dane grabbed me by the shoulders, pulled me to him and gave me a hug .In fact, for a moment, I thought he was going to kiss me. I held my breath, waiting, wanting that kiss—No! I shook my head and stepped back, out of his arms.

When I could talk without looking at him, I gave him the good news about Sonya's offer to help us out with Misty the next day.

He hadn't reserved a rental horse trailer yet, he told me and when I finally looked up again, I saw the relieved look on his face, probably that an experienced horseperson would be with us.

And then, because I felt exhausted and he admitted to it too, Dane said he needed to head home and get some sleep before our next busy day. I helped him pick up the tools and materials left over and put them in the truck bed.

As I lay in bed that night, trying to sleep, nervous about the next day, I thought how much my life had changed in a week. As well as the new job, starting tomorrow I would be responsible for taking care of a horse in my backyard—something I had dreamed of for as long as I could remember. And for the first time in a long time, there was a man—a wonderful man—in my life. Even though he shouldn't be.

CHAPTER NINE

Monday morning, I was sore from all the work I had done over the weekend. As I limped in, Olga told me with her usual smirk—probably happy to be the bearer of bad news—that Mrs. Braxton wanted to see me.

Uh-oh. Had someone seen Dane and me together that weekend? Could this be the end of my short career in the retirement living business?

I hurried down the hall to my office, tossed my coat onto a chair, and then walked slowly to Mrs. Braxton's office, going over excuses in my head, rehearsing what I'd say.

"Good morning, Micah. "She smiled. How was your weekend?"

Okay, this was definitely it. "Uh...I...fine," I answered, waiting for the "we're going to have to let you go" speech.

"Great." She smiled again, then leaned forward in her chair."Tell me, Micah, have you ever worked for a retirement home before?"

"Well, no...but my great-aunt was in one when I was little and we visited her there a couple times"—I'd told Lee that too—"but I've worked in marketing for several years. "

"Oh, sales," she said, sitting back with a satisfied smile, as though that might make up for my lack of experience in elder care.

"Well, no, not really...though sales is one form of marketing. "When she raised her eyebrows, I continued. "Actually, I'm more of a writer—ads, brochures, newsletters, direct mail, surveys...things like that. And promotions. I've handled a lot of events." I felt as though I was going through the interview for the job again...the interview I *should* have had. I suspected she was much more savvy about marketing than Lee.

"This job is probably not like any place you've ever worked, then. A big portion of our customers, the people we have to please, already *live* here. Until recently, Golden Valley got most of their referrals and their business from them. Residents told their friends about this place, their *home*, how much they liked it here, and why their friends would too.

"For years, Golden Valley had long waiting lists to get in. People got on the list knowing by the time they were ready to move in, there would be a spot here for them. But that has changed. We have a lot of competition. That's why we need to grow Golden Valley. And that's why the board of directors hired me. For now, or until we hire a Marketing Director, you and I will be a team. I want us to meet at least once a week...say, Monday mornings? At that time, we will discuss our strategy. You need more than Olga can teach you. I'm going to have you meet with a friend of mine, a top salesperson in his field. Do you know much about closing a sale?"

I shook my head.

"If I had more time, which I don't, I'd teach you myself. We need to get you up and running. As you know, we have several vacancies right now."

I nodded. Boy, *did* I. It had me worried too. Olga, I'm sure, had delighted in telling me that I was responsible for bringing in the majority of Golden Valley's income—though when I mentioned this to Terri, she said that the nursing center brought in a good deal of the income too. Still, I felt the weight of that responsibility on my shoulders.

"This building is old and hasn't been updated in years," Mrs. Braxton continued. "That's why the board wants to remodel, modernize—for now, to attract new residents, and for the generations to come."

I'd heard about this a bit from some of the more outspoken residents and Terri. Some of them were unhappy about the vacancies, afraid it would make their rent go up to make up for the lost income, and others complained about the changes to the building to come."But what about the people who already live here? Some residents have told me they moved here because they like it the way it is. They don't want it to change."

"Well if we don't make some changes, this community won't stay afloat," she snorted. "They'll just have to get used to it." She turned to her computer and typed something. "That's all the time I have for now. We'll meet again next Monday," she said briskly.

I sighed with relief as I walked back to my office.

The rest of the day went surprisingly well. I rented my first apartment. It was a great feeling. Finally,

I was earning my way. And I'd done it on my own, without coaching. Perhaps even better, I didn't have Olga dogging me.

Dane called me and said that he'd talked with someone in the horse rescue organization. "She said I needed to call Animal Control or the sheriff first, and then they can get involved. I'll do that next."

"Okay. Guess what?" I couldn't wait till I saw him later to tell him the good news. "I rented an apartment!"

"I think we should celebrate. I could feed Misty for you so you wouldn't have to change your clothes, and then we could go out for dinner. Whad'ya say?"

"You've already taken me to breakfast and bought lunch and dinner—" I started to protest but he interrupted.

"Breakfast, yeah, but lunch and dinner were just takeout and home delivery, so that doesn't count. Besides, this one's on Gramps. He's so grateful you agreed to take care of Misty. He was hoping we could stop by tonight before we leave. He'd like to tell you some things about her."

What excuse could I make now? I needed some

time to think. "Yeah, I'd like to talk to him about her. But maybe if you talk to him before tonight, you shouldn't tell him I'll stop by. It's been a really busy day and I have a lot of paperwork to do and people to talk to before I leave." It was the best I could do on the spur of the moment, and at least it gave me some time to think up a reason not to stop by. But Dane seemed to accept my explanation.

"Oh. Well okay. See you later."

The rest of the afternoon as I worked, I wondered what I could say that would keep me out of trouble once more.

Fortunately, my problem turned into not a problem when unbeknownst to Dane, his aunt Marcy had scheduled a doctor appointment for Carl. A cabulance was coming to get him and Marcy would follow in her car, with Dane's dad. I'd stopped wearing my outdoor clothes to work since Dane insisted he could pick me up at my place and take me home, without dropping me off at the bottom of the hill. He wouldn't admit that it was out of his way and said it gave him a good chance to see Misty and tell his grandfather about her the next morning. "But he'd still like to see you," Dane told me later when we were at the upscale restaurant he'd chosen.

I'd looked around now and then throughout our meal to make sure no one from Golden Valley was there. I felt pretty comfortable that we were safe, but I was glancing around again when I heard Dane's words, and choked on my food.

He patted my back. "Are you okay?" he asked with a concerned expression.

When I could speak again, I said, "Some-something just went down the wrong way." I wiped the tears from my eyes with my napkin. I couldn't have planned the distraction better.

"So, have you heard anything about your car?" Dane asked after we finished eating and he sipped the refill of his coffee the waitress brought before she cleared our dishes and brought the bill. "Is your insurance company going to fix it, or was it a total loss? It didn't look that bad to me, but I didn't look under the hood. Gramps said I was too busy saving a damsel in distress." He laughed.

"Um..."

"Yeah, I know, kinda corny, huh?"

I knew then I couldn't put it off any longer. "I've been meaning to talk to you about that." I hesitated. "My insurance company will pay to fix the car, but it will take about a month and I don't have rental car insurance," I blurted out in one breath. I just wanted to get it over with.

"Oh. Yeah, a month is a long time to be without a car...especially when you live in the country. You probably don't even have a bus system out there, do you?"

I shook my head.

"I don't mind taking you to work and back." He smiled. "In fact, I like it."

We gazed into each other's eyes for awhile until I turned and looking away, I replied,
"Are you sure? You won't think I'm taking advantage of you?"

"I'm the one who took advantage of you."

I turned back at that and raised an eyebrow at him. "I don't see how *that* could be possible."

"Asking you to board Gramp's horse."

"Are you kidding? You made a lifelong dream

possible."

CHAPTER TEN

I'd taken a few pictures of Misty in her new home and planned to send them to Dane's phone so he could show them to Carl, but since I hadn't figured out a way to get out of seeing him again—and endangering my job—I printed them out. Then I took some of my own pictures out of their frames and put Misty's photos in them. I thought Carl might enjoy having pictures of Misty on the walls or the bedside table, in his room. She looked so cute and festive in her green blanket with its red trim.

While Dane parked his car Tuesday morning, I glanced furtively around for anyone I knew, punched in the code and let myself in the back entrance. Scanning the corridors as I quietly walked through the nursing care wing, I slipped into Carl's room, glad to see he was awake.

"Hey Carl, it's Micah. Do you remember me? I brought some pictures of Misty for you. Do you want to see them now?" When he nodded, I pulled them out of my backpack, handed them to him, and then sat down next to the bed. He'd smiled when I walked in, but positively beamed when he looked at each framed photo.

"Thaankk youu," he said slowly, with tears in his eyes. I had to look away to keep my eyes from misting up too.

Shortly after that, Dane arrived and looked at the photos. He reminded his grandfather that Carl wanted to tell me some things about Misty.

Carl was silent for a moment as though trying to remember. "She loves app-pulls."

"I'll get a bag of 'em," Dane said, looking at his grandfather and then at me.

When Carl didn't say anything more to me, I stood up. But before I could leave, he reached for my hand. Then he turned and looked at Dane. "Sheeze a good gurrl. I l-like hurr."

The rest of my day was extremely busy. I spent much of my time on the phone answering questions about Golden Valley. One thing I heard over and over was, why did we not allow pets to live there? I made excuses, not really clear on the subject myself.

In the afternoon, I had two appointments to show the available apartments. The first was with a friendly couple. They seemed to really like the apartment I showed them, but said they had a couple other places to look at before they made a decision. I hoped they chose Golden Valley. I would enjoy having them there.

The next appointment was with a mother and daughter. The apartment was for the mother, and she seemed quite enthused about living there. The daughter was a different story. She just followed along, not saying much. It was when we came back to my office to discuss the details, that I felt tension in the room.

After I explained the costs, the daughter blurted out, "Well, I can see there won't be any inheritance for me!" She stood up, and stalked out of the office.

I felt bad for her poor mother who looked terribly sad and stressed. She hurriedly stood, gathering up her coat and purse. I handed the information packet to her, hoping she would somehow talk some sense into her daughter.

We started down the hall to the lobby where the younger woman waited. "It's your choice, you know. You need to think about yourself," I told the distraught woman.

"I know, I know," she said sadly.

But I doubted that she would. Why did my grandparents' generation feel the need to leave something for their children? Last week, some longtime residents moved out, saying they couldn't stay there in good conscience, knowing they needed to provide for their adult son the rest of their lives. Others wanted to send their grandkids to college. If so, they were lucky grandkids. My grandparents had long since passed away and in fact, two of them I barely remembered. I wondered if my generation would be so compassionate when we were that age.

I was feeling kinda down, and certainly tired, by the time I joined Dane in the car that night after work. But he was in a good mood, it seemed. He talked about his grandfather and how glad Carl was that Dane and I had moved Misty...and then I guess I zoned out, thinking my own thoughts, when I heard him say the word,

"Thanksgiving."

"I'm sorry, what did you say?"

"What are you doing for Thanksgiving?"

"I'm not...I don't know yet. When is it, anyway?"

"Micah, it's in two days!"

"Oh yeah, sure, I knew that. Just kidding." I laughed so he wouldn't think I'd lost my mind, but I really had forgotten. Maybe I just wanted to put it out of my mind.

"I just thought you might be at Golden Valley."

"Oh, no, I have that day off. I do have to work the next day, though. I'm told it's a busy day with adult children in town, wanting to look at places for parents while they're here visiting.

"Well, since Gramps is there, just about everyone in our family—my sisters, Aunt Marci and Uncle Dave and a couple of their kids—are going there for the Thanksgiving dinner for residents and their families.

"That's nice," I said half-heartedly. I knew what I was doing, I'd be home alone. Since Mom planned to be away, I wouldn't be spending the holiday with her this year. If my friend Jasmine knew, she'd invite me to her parents' for dinner, but I didn't want that.

"Would you like to join us?"

What? I hoped I didn't look as started as I felt. If only I could tell him what I really wanted to say—that I would love to. "Oh, I couldn't...I mean, it's your time with your family."

"Gramps asked me if you'd be there. And you could meet my mom and dad. Everyone's very grateful for what you did for Misty. And you know *I'd* like you to be there."

How could I turn him down? But I had to. Sneaking rides with Dane and into Carl's room to visit was bad enough, but no way could I appear in the dining room with them and their family. If only I could say "yes," but I had to lie again. It was getting harder and harder to do.

"I'd love to, really, but I promised my mom we'd spend the day together."

"I thought you said you didn't know what you were doing?" Did I detect some suspicion in his voice? Or was it just my feelings of guilt?

"That's true. I left it up to Mom. I don't know

what she has planned."

"Oh, I see." This time he just sounded disappointed. Maybe I had imagined the doubt in his voice after all. Oh, why was this happening? I'd finally met a great guy who appeared to like me too, and all I could do was try to avoid getting together with him. What had I ever done to deserve this?

The rest of the week—all two days until the holiday—flew by. By then, I'd met with all the managers or department directors and learned the process to get an apartment ready for a new resident once I'd rented it.

The maintenance department included a painter who painted the apartment for each new resident, according to the wall and trim colors they picked. We had a carpet installer on contract who came and put in the carpet the resident had chosen, and our own crew who did any repairs or modifications to plumbing and electrical. And then I spoke to the housekeeping department who thoroughly cleaned the apartment just prior to move-in day. We even had one or two moving companies that I could recommend if needed.

Then I met with the people who took care of

and/or entertained the residents—nursing, food service, activities, exercise coordinator and the hair salon owner.

Olga had stressed to me the importance of knowing *everything* about Golden Valley—just as she claimed she did—so that when potential residents and their families asked questions, I would have the answers. Needless to say, I took lots of notes.

"Have a great Thanksgiving with your mom, whatever you two decide to do," Dane told me when he dropped me off at my place Wednesday night. Normally, he stayed a bit and visited with Misty for awhile so he could tell Carl about her the next morning. But that night, he said he had to go to the store and get some things his mother asked him to pick up. Even though they were having dinner at Golden Valley, his mother wanted to make her special pies.

"Thanks, Dane. You and your family have a great time, too. I hope you like the dinner. I took a peek at the menu and it looked good," I told him, forcing a smile.

CHAPTER ELEVEN

I told myself I would sleep in a little late on Thanksgiving morning, but knowing Misty was waiting for her breakfast, I pulled some sweatpants on over my nightgown, shoved my feet into my tall rubber boots and grabbed my heavy coat off the hooks by the door.

I thought she might be waiting for me with a big neigh, but she stood by the neighbors' side of the fence with her head over it, having a conversation with Caleb—or so it appeared. There was a lot of blowing and snorting. I even showed her the apple. That usually did the trick when I wanted her attention, but not this time.

"Okay, suit yourself. And I was going to give you a treat this morning, because its Thanksgiving," I told her as I walked to the barn. But she stayed by the fence as I put a flake of hay in the manger and grain in a rubber dish. I checked the water trough as I walked back to the house to make sure the floating heater was working, and used that opportunity to scoop some debris out of the water.

I decided not to go back to bed, but didn't get dressed either. Instead, I picked up a new paperback bestseller I hadn't had time to read, and plopped down on the sofa. I stopped to watch the Macy's Thanksgiving Day Parade for awhile, and then went back to my book. The weather pretty much suited my mood—it rained most of the day.

When it came time for my dinner, I headed to the refrigerator, pulled the frozen meal out of the freezer, and switched on the stove to preheat it. But when I opened the box, I stopped and looked at the picture of turkey, gravy, potatoes and cranberries, and suddenly my brain told my stomach, "no." I turned the oven off again, put the frozen dinner back in the freezer, and pulled a box of popcorn out of the cupboard instead.

As I waited for the bag of corn kernels to pop, I glanced out the kitchen window to the pasture. Misty still stood by the neighbors' fence, though Caleb was no longer there. Maybe she was bored. The microwave dinged and I pulled the bag out, then walked back to the window to watch Misty as I ate. She kept turning her head around and biting at her side. It wasn't warm or sunny, so I didn't think flies would be bothering her. I decided I'd better get dressed and go out to check.

By the time I was dressed for the cold, rain and mud, and looked out the window once again, Misty was no longer standing. She lay on the ground, rolling from side to side. I raced out the door, down the stairs and across the yard to the pasture gate. I knew that horses rolled. It was like taking a bath for them. But something wasn't right, and I didn't know what to do.

I turned around and ran back to the house, where I grabbed my cell phone. Scrolling through my contacts, I pulled up Dane's phone number. I hated to call him while he was having Thanksgiving dinner with his family, but I wanted Carl to know and hopefully tell me what to do.

When Dane answered, he was laughing. "Hi, Micah, Happy Thanksgiving."

"Yes, you too," I said but I wasn't in the mood for niceties. "Dane, I think something is wrong with Misty," I blurted out.

"Uh-oh." His tone turned serious. It sounded as

though he held the phone away and I heard him talking to someone. Then he came back on the line and said, "What is she doing? What are her symptoms?"

While I talked, I'd gone back out to the pasture, opened the gate and walked to the barn. I looked in the manger and saw that Misty hadn't eaten any of her morning food.

"She hasn't eaten, she's been biting her side, she looks sweaty and she's been rolling, but she just got up again. Now, she's pawing the ground."

I heard Dane talking again, but not into the phone. Then he said, "Micah, I'm going to call the vet, and then I'll head over there. Can I give the vet your phone number in case he has any questions?"

"Of course. Do you have any idea what it could be?"

"Gramps said it sounds like colic. Oh, just a minute." He spoke away from the phone again, then came back on the line. "Do you think you could walk her around the pasture while you wait for the vet? I can relieve you when I get there."

"Sure, I can do that. I'll do it now."

"Thanks, Micah. I'll be there soon," Dane said.

I fought to hold back tears, but they fell anyway. Why hadn't I checked on Misty sooner, instead of feeling sorry for myself and holing up inside all day? What must Dane and his family think of me? That I was totally inept? As soon as Misty was well again, they'd probably take her away, to some fancy stable with real horsepeople who knew what they were doing.

And Dane...he wouldn't want anything to do with me. I should feel glad about that, but I couldn't. Even though I could lose my job, I found it harder and harder to act indifferent. I liked being around him too much. I just kept thinking that if Carl got better and went back home, and Misty was here, maybe Dane would still come to visit. At least we'd have that connection. But now, it felt as though all my hopes had gone down the drain.

As I thought all this, Misty and I walked the fence line. Most of the time, she seemed willing, but twice, she stopped and wouldn't move. "Come on, Misty," I pleaded with her. This is for your own good. You need to help me out here."

Finally, I heard a vehicle pull into the driveway,

but I didn't want to stop and find out whether it was the vet or Dane. And if it *was* Dane, I couldn't let him see me crying. I quickly brushed the tears away, and kept walking with Misty.

"Micah? Have you heard from the vet?" I heard Dane call to me.

"No," I called back, then waited for him to reach us.

"How is she?"

"I don't know. We've been walking pretty much ever since I talked to you, except for a couple times when she stopped. At least she hasn't tried to lie down again."

"You've done a terrific job. Here, you rest and I'll walk her for a while."

I handed the lead rope to him and watched him walk away with Misty. Then I blew on my numbed fingers, trying to warm them up. I'd forgotten my gloves in my haste to get outside. I contemplated going inside to get them, but decided I'd better stick around in case Misty wanted to stop again. So I shoved my hands in my pockets instead and watched. I heard Dane's cell phone ring and when he stopped to answer it, I quickly walked over to join them.

"It's the vet," he said holding the phone away from his mouth for a second, and handed the lead rope to me. After a while, he said, "Okay, thank you Dr. Davis. We'll keep walking her, then. "He pressed the end call button, and then typed in another number. When he started talking—I assumed to his family—I tugged on the rope.

"C'mon, Misty, you heard. More walking, "I told her. When I opened my mouth to speak, I noticed how tight my teeth had been clenched. My jaw ached. It could have been from the cold, but I suspected tension instead. I couldn't help thinking how disgusted Dane and his family must be with me. Dane was just too polite to show it. And Carl...I couldn't bear to think about how much I must have disappointed him. He'd been so happy his beloved horse was in good hands...Ha!

Dane came up beside us, just as Misty reached out in an attempt to snag the branch off a bush. "Sorry about the calls. After I talked to the vet, I called my dad to update Gramps. The vet said it sounded like a mild case of colic, and the walking was all she needed but he's going to come out and check on her. He had another emergency call, which is why we didn't hear from him earlier. He's on his way here now."

"Oh, that's wonderful news! I'm so glad. She *does* seem better. Before, she wasn't hungry at all, but now she's trying to grab grass and even bushes as we pass by."

Dane laughed. "That's right. Gramps calls trail riding Misty's opportunity to dine at the salad bar. I guess that's what she's trying to do now.

The vet finally arrived and confirmed that she probably did have colic, but she was okay, although I shouldn't give her any grain until the next day, and keep an eye on her for awhile. As his truck pulled out of the driveway, Dane said, "Are you ready for a piece of Mom's pumpkin pie?" He pulled a whole pie out of his car. "She said this one is for you."

"Really? I *love* pumpkin pie. *"Maybe it wasn't the worst Thanksgiving I'd ever had after all.*

CHAPTER TWELVE

Dane had assured me the night before that he planned to go to work the next day. He said he wanted to catch up on paperwork he couldn't get done during the regular work week. And since the crew and office staff had taken a four-day holiday, he could work without interruptions.

I wasn't sure what to expect at Golden Valley. I didn't have any appointments scheduled, but there could be walk-ins, so it might be quite busy. At least Olga and Mrs. Braxton weren't supposed to be there. I'd learned that little tidbit on Wednesday when I overheard them talking just outside Mrs. B's office.

As I walked in the lobby, I saw several large boxes lining the walls, and the maintenance crew had a large dolly loaded with more.

"Tom, what are all these boxes for?" I asked.

"Christmas decorations," he answered with a grimace.

It seemed a little early to me, but it was Black Friday for the retail stores, so I supposed I shouldn't be surprised.

When I sat down at my desk and opened up the computer to read my emails, I saw one from Mrs. Braxton. Although it wasn't to me specifically, it was to all departments heads, which included me until a marketing director was hired. The gist of it was that whenever we weren't "otherwise occupied," she expected us to help decorate the tree and the lobby.

Christmas hadn't been a big deal to me after my parents divorced. Mom tried, but funds were limited. My dad usually sent a check from wherever he lived, though the amount varied depending on how big his commissions were, I later learned from Mom. He was a salesman, which considering my job at Golden Valley, seemed especially ironic. Obviously, his aptitude hadn't been passed on to me. I suppose I may have been more like my mother, though hers was sewing and mine was writing. Anyway, we both had good imaginations, whereas Dad's skills lay in numbers, something that definitely wasn't *my* forte.

My grandfather and aunts also sent something for Christmas when they could, but then Grandpa passed away, and after we kids grew up, my cousins and I no longer had gift exchanges and our parents just exchanged gift among themselves if at all.

I didn't get too excited about the holidays anymore and putting up Christmas decorations wasn't really my thing. I certainly didn't decorate my own home.

Funny thing, though, my best friend Jasmine, was just the opposite. Her family celebrated big, and when she moved into her own apartment, she did too. It wasn't that I didn't believe in Christmas and all it stood for, I did. I even went to Christmas Eve services with Jasmine and her family most years. But why decorate my own place when no one saw it? And Mom always made sure we had a tree of some sort—although usually pretty small. In fact, they seemed to be getting smaller and smaller now that I no longer lived with her. Last year, it sat on the old sideboard that she'd inherited from her mother. I suspected this year's would be even smaller, until maybe someday—like me—she wouldn't bother at all.

After I'd read all my emails and taken care of every little thing I could think of, I couldn't put it off any longer, and forced myself to walk out to the lobby. Much to my surprise—and dismay—there I found Mrs. Braxton, in street clothes, directing some of the maintenance crew, who stood on tall ladders, putting up a *huge*, artificial Christmas tree. It looked like something I'd seen in FAO Schwarz, the toy store I'd visited with my parents in downtown Seattle when I was a kid. I remember being fascinated by that place, with the fifteen foot, bronze, waving teddy bear out front. It seemed to me then that *everything* was big. Of course, the toys were way too expensive for my family's budget. Maybe they were for most families too, because I heard the store closed in Seattle after a few years.

"Oh, Micah! There you are. Could you take these caroling figures and put them on the table outside the business office?" Mrs. Braxton gestured toward a box on the floor.

I smiled weakly. "Sure." I walked over and grabbed a box of foot tall, old-time caroler figurines, and carried them down the hall to a table covered in "snow." I picked them out of the box one by one and then set them with the other figures someone had already placed there.

When I went back to the lobby, the tree was almost all put together, and one of the guys was already pulling lights out of a box and plugging them into an electrical outlet, while another one began stringing them along the lower boughs. Looking around, I saw two small children standing next to the tree. And then I did a double take. The children weren't real, they were actually life-size Victorian figures made to look like toddlers staring up at the tree on Christmas morning. I saw another box labeled *Toy Train,* which I guessed would go under the tree.

Meanwhile, Mrs. Braxton had moved on to other boxes labeled, *Tree Ornaments,* and pulled out a large glass orb. "Micah," she called, beckoning to me with the hand not holding the ornament by its hook. So I walked over. "Now, when Will gets all the lights on the tree, you can start putting the ornaments on....Oh, and when that's done, I want the nativity put over there on that side table."

And so my day went, occasionally interrupted by my real job of answering calls and giving tours to drop-ins.

On the way home, I asked Dane about his day.

"Pretty quiet, thank goodness. I got a lot done. How about yours?"

"Ohh," I groaned. "Busy."

"Did you rent another apartment?" he asked with interest.

"Well, no, not that kind of busy. I spent most of my time being an elf."

"What?" He turned in his seat and gave me a quizzical look.

"I felt as though I was in Santa's workshop—something like that—or maybe, decorating a department store window for Christmas."

Dane just stared at me. Good thing we were stopped at a light.

"My boss came in on her day off, and we decorated the lobby for Christmas," I explained.

It was Dane's turn to groan then. "Oh boy. *That's* what I forgot to do. I had this nagging feeling I was supposed to do something for Mom, and now I remember what. She wanted me to get the Christmas decorations out of the storeroom so she could sort through them and see what needed to be thrown out, what to keep, and what she'll need to buy for the office this year. Man...now I'll have to go back into the office tomorrow too!"

I felt for him. I certainly wouldn't want to go to my workplace on my days off.

"Mom waits till December first at least to decorate the house, but she lets Dad wait till the second weekend to get the tree. If you get them too early, the needles are dropping by Christmas. In fact, one year, we had to take the tree down before the night was over. It was so dry, it was a fire hazard. "He laughed .

"They still get a real tree every year? Seems like everyone uses artificial ones these days."

"At work, yeah, but Mom likes the smell of a real tree, she says. And she wants it fresh, not one that's been 'sitting on a lot for who knows how long.' So my folks make a big deal out of going to a tree farm and cutting one down. Their house has vaulted ceilings and Mom always picks out the biggest tree she can find. That's why I go along...to help Dad carry it to the truck, and then get it into the house. When do you start decorating for Christmas?"

"I...uh...well, I don't. Mom always has a tree, so with just me alone, why bother?"

"Oh." He sounded disappointed, so I changed the subject.

"Have you heard from the horse rescue organization?"

"No, but they said it can take a while to get things moving. I think first they try to work with the horse owner, see if maybe they just need a little help caring for the horses with food and other necessities."

"It looked like more than that to me," I said indignantly. "Maybe we should call them again and see what's happening? Remember, my neighbor Sonya offered to help too. She said sometimes they need assistance hauling horses and she's willing to do that with her trailer. And I'd be happy to help in any way I could. Maybe I could go with her since I don't have a car right now."

"Or we could go together. I could use one of the

company trucks to haul stuff."

"That would be great! But first, I think we should find out *how* we can help."

By then, we had reached my home. It seemed darker than usual. "You could use some more light around here," Dane observed.

"Yeah, I must've forgotten to turn on the porch light. Let me see," I answered, fumbling for my keys as we climbed the steps. Once inside, I flipped the switch by the door. "Nope, the bulb must be burned out. I'll go get another one."

When I brought the bulb to the door, Dane reached out for it and said, "Here, I'll do it while you change into your barn clothes. Meet you outside." I saw him walking around the yard. He seemed to be pacing something off and then whipped a measuring tape out of his pocket.

I joined him outside shortly after that, but before I could ask what he was up to, he blurted out, "What you really need is a dusk-to-dawn light in the yard on a pole and one on the barn as well. If your landlord won't okay the yard light, I could at least put one on the barn. You need more light than what's in the barn and on your porch. And out here, with no streetlights, it's so dark."

"Yes, but like you said, the landlord may not go along with it."

"Tell you what, if he objects to the expense, I'll do it all at no cost to you or him, then. In fact, just tell him you'll have it done, no charge to him."

"But—"I started to protest, but he cut me off.

"Micah, you're boarding Misty here. You need the light."

"Yes, but, you're making all these improvements to this place and there's no way you'll get reimbursed. I can't and I'm sure the owner won't. Can you at least reuse the materials somewhere if I have to move out someday?"

"You worry too much," Dane told me with a laugh and a light punch on my arm. But he must have seen I wasn't smiling. "Yeah, sure. I can do that."

"Good. I'll call the landlord."

CHAPTER THIRTEEN

This time, my landlord didn't answer when I called. Not knowing when he'd call back, Dane decided not to wait around and left after we'd fed Misty and spent some time with her.

"Call me when you hear what he says, and I can get the materials. I'd like to get started on it tomorrow if you don't mind. And if you have something else to do, I'd be working outside and wouldn't get in your way."

"Actually, I do. My friend is coming to visit. But if you need help, maybe we could reschedule."

"Friend?" Dane frowned.

"Yes, I do have a friend or two, at least in Seattle. I just don't get to see them much with my new job and the weather, and of course, lack of a car. And then, Jasmine's been so busy—"

"Jasmine? Oh, you mean a *female* friend." He sounded relieved. Was he worried I might have a boyfriend? Hmm. "No, I won't need any help. You deserve some time off, anyway."

"Are you sure?" I couldn't bear to think of something happening to him, climbing ladders and who knows what other dangerous things, while I went off and had fun.

"Yeah, I'm sure."

The next morning, I heard the big diesel pulling into the driveway, followed by a larger, flatbed truck with what appeared to be a telephone pole on the bed. I'd called Dane after I heard from my landlord late the night before. The owner said again, he didn't care what I did to the place as long as it was an improvement. He also reminded me that the extra light would use more electricity, and I assured him again that I would pay for it.

I stepped out onto the porch, surprised to see the sunshine. Earlier, when I fed Misty, it looked as though we were going to have rain. I'd watched clouds scudding across the sky, but the wind must have swept away the rain clouds because it was now definitely a blue sky, sunny day, my favorite kind of weather in my favorite season of the year.

"Hey, Dane," I called. "Looks like you brought the good weather with you." He and a man with salt and pepper hair and beard were standing by the trucks, talking. When I called out, they headed over to the porch.

"Hi, Micah. Looks as though your friend isn't here yet. I don't see a car."

"It's a little early for Jasmine. She always runs late anyway." I smiled and looked at the other man as I said it.

"Dane?" the older man said, turning to him and raising his eyebrows.

"Oh, sorry. Micah, I'd like you to meet my dad, Chip."

"Mr. Andersen, I should have recognized you. You look so much like Carl." Actually, he looked like Dane too. Both of them were tall, though Dane looked a bit taller. Carl was in bed the times I'd visited, so I didn't know if he was tall too, but all three had the same smiles, and the same crinkly, bright blue eyes. And though Carl's hair was all white, Chip had the same dark hair as Dane's, mixed in with the gray.

"So I've been told. I'm actually Carl Jr., but it

was too confusing when we worked together, and when somebody called me a 'chip off the old block,' it stuck." He laughed.

"Yeah, and the funny thing is, Mom told me that Dad had just fired the guy and he was comparing Dad to Gramps." Dane and his dad looked at each other then and laughed even harder. I could see that the two men had a great relationship and I felt a sudden twinge of regret that I didn't have that with my dad. But the feeling quickly disappeared as I listened to their good-natured teasing.

Then Chip stopped abruptly and turned to me. "Sorry, we carry on like this all the time. So before your friend comes, I just wanted to tell you that I'm delighted to finally meet the young lady my son and Pops talk about so much and—"

I started to interrupt, but he waved a hand to stop me.

—"and you're every bit as pretty and kind as I expected," he finished.

I felt my face grow warm. I wasn't used to compliments—genuine ones, anyway. But before I could deny his words, I heard a nicker and turning, spied Misty at the gate,

"Hey, there she is," Chip said after he turned around too. "Did you bring the apples, Son? I promised Pops I'd give her one for him."

When Dane walked back to the truck to get them, I laughed and told Chip, "You know if you do that, you'll have another helper out there. She'll follow you around like a puppy."

And that's exactly what she did, I noticed later as I looked out my kitchen window while rinsing dishes and loading them into the dishwasher. It was nearly noon by then, and Jasmine hadn't yet arrived. At least she'd texted to tell me she was running late. I wasn't a bit surprised.

Finally, I heard a car in the driveway, scattering gravel as it came to an abrupt stop. It had to be Jasmine. I grabbed my purse and opening the door, stepped out onto the porch.

"I'm ready if you are," I called to her.

"She opened the door and stepped out of the car. "Wow. This looks like a construction site. What are those two gorgeous men on ladders doing down by the barn?"

"I'll tell you about it at lunch, unless you need to make a pit stop first."

"Might be a good idea. I drank this whole thing on the drive here." She held up an oversized coffee travel mug.

As I waited, I watched Dane and Chip at work. As far as I could tell, they'd worked on the wiring first, and now were hanging the outdoor light on the front of the barn, way up above the hay loft. Their ladders were tall, but it was still a reach, and I shuddered to think what would happen if one of them fell. I should be down there holding the ladders for them. But just as I put my purse down and reached for my rubber boots on the boot tray by the door, Jasmine said, "Ready? Let's go. I'm anxious to hear what's going on here."

I picked my purse up again and said, "Sure. Let's go." I told myself I didn't need to worry about them. They must be used to doing that kind of work, climbing ladders all the time...except Chip probably didn't do much actual construction work himself anymore at his age...

"Micah, come on, I'm starving!"

As I climbed into Jasmine's low-slung, sporty car, I wondered if I should let Dane and Chip know I was leaving but didn't want to startle them by calling out. As Jasmine drove off, chatting away, I couldn't help wishing I hadn't made lunch plans for the weekend.

"So, tell me everything," Jasmine said when we sat down at the restaurant and scanned the menus the waitress had given us. "I can't believe you've been holding out on me."

I raised an eyebrow and gave my friend my best pained look.

"Oh, don't give me that." Jasmine raised one brow too. "I'm the one who taught you how to do that in Mr. Barlow's boring English class, in case you've forgotten."

"You did?"

"Ha ha, you're avoiding the subject. Now, dish."

"Oh, all right."

Fifteen minutes later, I'd told her all about Dane,

Carl, Misty, Chip, Olga and Mrs. Braxton, and the waitress was setting our dishes of food down on the table before us. I hoped that my "starving" friend would dig into her food and leave me a few minutes of peace. I even picked up my fork and began to eat, hoping she'd do the same, but no such luck.

"Maybe your boss is right. It *is* a business, after all."

It wasn't what I'd expected to hear, and I stared at her in shock. "You're supposed to be on my side!" I said indignantly and put down my fork.

"I *am* on your side. I'm just saying what you already know and don't want to admit."

"Yeah, I suppose..."

"You've always been a softie, ya know." My friend gave me a knowing look. "Always sticking up for the underdog."

"I suppose," I said again.

"Well, as I see it, you have two options. You can either make up some excuse and tell Dane you can't ride to and from work with him anymore and stop worrying about getting caught or tell him the truth."

"I–I can't."

"Why not? Are you worried his family will take the horse away? I know you've always wanted one."

"No...well yeah, that too, but that's not it."

"Are you worried about how you will get to work—though why you moved somewhere so far out in the country that it doesn't have bus service, I don't get." She shook her head

"No...although yeah, that is a problem right now without my car, but that's not it."

"Are you afraid you won't see him anymore if you don't have a reason to see him every day? By the way, I can't see that happening. From all you've told me, this guy likes you, Micah."

"That's the problem! I like him too. And if I tell him what I've been doing, sneaking around because I'm not supposed to have anything to do with him, what will he—and his family—think of me? They have a business too. They would expect their employees to follow the rules. At first, I did ride with him because I trusted him and I needed a way to get to work, that's true, but now—"

"Now, you don't know how to tell him the truth without losing him," Jasmine finished for me.

I nodded.

"But you're risking losing your job, and girlfriend, you really need this job."

"I know."

CHAPTER FOURTEEN

Somebody had been busy over the weekend. A huge wreath hung on the wall behind the reception desk. Pots of red, pink and white poinsettia plants graced the desk and tables in the lobby. And the work continued. Tom and his crew walked past me with strings of lights which they carried outside. That explained the ladders I'd seen leaning against the sides of the building.

And when I walked into my office, I found another poinsettia on my desk, and a CD in a white sleeve marked "Christmas Carols." I figured either Olga or Mrs. Braxton must have placed it there. I'd been gradually bringing some of my things from home to make the office feel more like my own space than the previous marketing coordinator, including my old radio/CD player. It sat on the credenza behind my desk, in full view of anyone who walked in, not to mention those two eagle-eyed women.

Sure enough, when I logged on to the computer, there was an email from Mrs. B. She wrote that she couldn't meet with me (again) today, but had left the CD for me to play, at least during appointments, and maybe all day in case I had walk-ins. I liked Christmas carols as much as the next person—in fact, "O Holy Night" was my favorite. I got chills when I listened to it, it was so beautiful—but I hoped she didn't expect me to play that same CD over and over. I made a mental note to bring in some CDs of my own.

When I left work that night, I noticed the giant Christmas tree in the lobby glittered with tiny bright lights and shiny ornaments. Under the tree, someone had placed packages wrapped in pretty paper and sparkly bows, and when I walked out the doors to the street, green lights hung from the eaves of the building.

One thing I had been able to accomplish to keep my relationship with Dane less stressful, was to convince him to park somewhere on the street farther away from Golden Valley. I told him my coworkers would give me a bad time if they saw me in the car with a man and I'd never hear the end of it. He agreed and when he couldn't find parking close by, he'd send a text to let me know where to find him.

"Hi, how was your day?" I asked him when I got in the car.

"Well, I have some news," he said with a smile.

"Carl's going home?" I asked hopefully.

His smile faded. "No. I wish he was. In fact, he hasn't been progressing much lately. He kind of rallied for awhile on Thanksgiving, but this morning he was pretty quiet."

I really didn't know much about strokes. "I'm sorry to hear that." Dane looked so discouraged, I wished I'd never said anything and hurried to change the subject. "So what's the news?"

"I got a call from the rescue organization

"And?"

"Only a couple of the horses were actually boarders and belonged to families with daughters who had gone off to college. The parents didn't check on the horses, just sent in the monthly board, and weren't aware of the conditions there. They've moved the horses to a another boarding facility. The sheriff will check on them now and then to make sure the horses are being properly taken care of."

"I hope so!" I said indignantly. And the others?"

He sighed. "I wish I could say they were leaving immediately. Evidently, the owners fell on hard times and cannot afford to take care of them. The county is helping out right now with food until the rescue organization can get together a team of horse people and trailers to get them out of there." He hesitated. "The other thing is, they don't have enough places to keep that many horses."

"What do you mean? The rescue group facility is full?"

"Well, from what I learned today, it's kinda like kids going into foster homes instead of orphanages. Unlike some rescue groups I've read about in other counties or states, this one relies on foster families to keep the horses for awhile until they can be adopted. And evidently, right now, all the foster homes are full."

"They need to get them out of there. What can we do to help? Maybe I could keep one or two for awhile."

"Funny you should say that. After I got the phone call at the office, Dad said he couldn't help overhearing my end of the conversation and wondered what was going on. So I explained it to him, and he said the same thing. But it sounds like you'd need to prequalify.

"The woman with the horse rescue group said foster caregivers provide regular meals, turnout, grooming, blanketing, are there for veterinarian and horseshoeing appointments, and general care...I *think* that's what she said. She rattled it off, and I scribbled a few notes while we talked. But they'll pay for things like that, all you'd have to do is care for them."

"Whew," I said, relieved.

"Sooo...if that is something you want to do, Dad and I would like to help by getting your place set up. You'd need a couple more stalls in the barn, some cross-fencing—"he must have seen my raised eyebrow—"you know, a way to separate the horses? I mentioned it to Gramps, and he said they should be separated at first to see if they get along and definitely at meals."

"Yes, I think I do. I really want to help in some way if I can. Do you want to call the rescue group lady since you've talked to her, or should I?"

"I'll call her back tomorrow and see if she can come out this weekend. If so, business is slow for us right now, so I could definitely do some fencing and stalls this week." He pulled into my driveway just as he finished speaking. The yard and pasture were bathed in the bright glow of the dusk-to-dawn lights, almost as good as a full moon overhead

"I'm so glad you and your dad put the lights up. What a difference it makes. I feel a lot safer too. It was kinda creepy being out here at night before that."

"Glad to be of service, ma'am," Dane drawled and feigned tipping his wool cap in imitation of a cowboy.

"You need a cowboy hat," I mused aloud.

"Do you have one?"

"No...Wait! I *do*, or I did," I amended. "It was for a Halloween party a while ago. But since I moved here, I haven't unpacked all the boxes. Hmm, I'll have to dig it out. Anyway, we're talking about you," I reminded him with a laugh.

That night, I called Sonya to give her the status on the horse rescue. "Oh, I've been meaning to call you. Misty and Caleb had an adventure this afternoon. I don't know which one, but they broke a couple boards, and Misty stepped over the fence to join him. Looks like she was here most of the day. When I saw her in our pasture, I tried to get her to go back over the fence, but she wouldn't, so I left her here till I could get the boards nailed back up again. Then I walked her down the road to your place. Neither she nor Caleb were happy about it."

"Oh, Sonya, I'm, so sorry. I'll ask Dane if he can extend the wire for the electric fence along that side. We didn't think we needed it there. I have noticed that she and Caleb spend a lot of time talking over the fence. I hope this won't be a problem until he can get that wire up."

"Yeah, even though I only work a half day, it leaves them all morning after we leave to get into trouble. And sometimes I run errands on my way home, so it could be even later...I have an idea. Would you object to a gate between our two pastures? You could still have a hot wire along our fence, but make a break there and install a gate handle. Sure, would make it a lot easier to go back and forth."

"Sonya, that's a great idea! Really, it's okay with you? I'd sure feel a lot better being gone all day, knowing Misty wasn't trying to break through the fence and possibly getting injured."

"I'll see if Bob will take those boards back down later after they've both eaten their dinners."

"Okay, but first I'll call Dane and see if he can do the fencing. He was planning to come out tomorrow to do some work in the barn and on the fences before the horse rescue group comes out to see if I'm set up for foster care."

When I talked to Dane, he thought it was a great idea, and said he would be out the next morning after he dropped me off at Golden Valley and got a few supplies. I called Sonya back and told her to expect to see Dane working at my place during the day that week.

The next morning, I went out to feed Misty as usual in my sweats and rubber boots...and couldn't find her.

Panic.

I grabbed her halter and rope, walked back out of the barn and through the gap in Sonya and Bob's fence, happy to see Misty inside Caleb's open barn. She was helping herself to the hay in Caleb's trough, while he stood a distance away, stalks of hay hanging from the corner of his mouth.

"Misty, that's not your food!" I yelled, and she jumped back, either scared, surprised or guilty—possibly all three. She snorted and ran past Caleb, who calmly took her place at his feed trough. Oh, this wasn't working. What could I do? The boards were down on the fence, and I didn't have the time to put them back.

"Micah." I looked up and saw Sonya waving at me from the gate between her yard and the pasture. "Why don't you bring Misty's hay over here and put it in the other stall? They'll probably switch back and forth between stalls, but at least they'll both get their breakfast."

"I'm sorry about this. If you really don't mind, that sounds like the perfect solution for now. Thanks so much!"

I told Dane about it when he arrived about an

hour later.

"Gramps should get a good laugh out of this when I tell him—I hope. He hasn't been saying much about anything. Maybe it will cheer him up to learn Misty has a boyfriend."

I could hear the worry in his voice and patted his arm. "I hope so too."

CHAPTER FIFTEEN

I called Dane on my lunch break the next day.

"How's it going? Are Misty and Caleb getting along okay? No injuries?"

He laughed." Nah, they're fine. He's pretty mellow, just lets her do whatever she wants."

"Oh good." I breathed a sigh of relief.

"I did find something interesting in the barn, however. Did you ever notice something covered with a very dusty tarp, way in the back?"

"No. It's always so dark back there and with all those cobwebs and dirt...no, I didn't want to look."

"Too bad, because you would have discovered a...sleigh."

"A *sleigh*? Cool! What's it look like?"

"It seems to be in good shape. But if I try to describe it, I don't think I can do it justice, except that it's red. Can you wait till tonight to see it?"

"Couldn't you take a picture and send it to me?"

"I'll try, but as you said, it's pretty dark back in that corner."

"Oh, all right, I'll wait," I said reluctantly.

After we ended the call, I sent a text to Sonya. "Know anything about the sleigh in my barn?"

She sent one right back. "I have the harness for it."

Surprise, surprise.

"Really."

"Yup. Come over tonight. I'll tell you what I know about it."

"K."

Dane's texted me shortly before I left work. "Driving the truck."

If he hadn't told me ahead of time, I would have looked for the Subaru instead. Actually, I liked riding in the truck. It was a one-ton, with four-wheel drive, and though a little harder to climb into, I liked sitting up high. I could see more than riding in a car. Maybe that's why, as Dane drove us through town, I noticed the holiday banners on Main Street, the twinkling white lights in otherwise bare tree branches along the sidewalk, the red ribbon-bedecked wreaths on the old-fashioned lamp posts, shop windows decorated and lit in the darkness.

"Wow, this town really celebrates. All these lights and decorations are really cool. Does your mom have her house decorated for Christmas now?" I asked Dane,

"Yup. And this weekend we'll be getting the tree. Hope it doesn't rain. That kinda puts a damper on things." He grinned, and I laughed too at his wit. "Do you want to come with us?"

I did, but I shouldn't. So I asked, "Do you know when that woman from the horse rescue group is coming to check out my place?

"That's right. I have to get back to her tonight...She can meet with you Saturday morning."

"That works for me," I replied, hoping that would get me out of going with him and his parents to get the tree."

"Well, shoot. That's when Dad wants to get the tree. Maybe I could ask him—"

"No!" I knew what he was going to say. But he looked so startled when I stopped him, I hastened to add,

"It's not that I don't want to—I've never done anything like that and it sounds like fun—but I'm sure your mom is anxious to get her tree and that will give her time to decorate it. Maybe next year—" I stopped, in shock at what had just slipped out.

Dane didn't say anything for awhile, then, "Yeah, you're right. It will take her all weekend. And then she'll want to make the wreaths too for the house and the office."

I felt a little hurt, but tried not to show it when he made no comment about next year. But maybe he felt he'd been rebuffed by me too many times. Maybe he thought this was all business for me. If only I could tell him the truth—that he was the nicest, sweetest, most handsome, caring, wonderful man I'd ever known.

When we got to my place, I was anxious to see the sleigh and headed right to the barn. I flipped on the light inside. Even with the outside lights, it was still pretty dark in there except the area just around the one light. The glow from Dane's big flashlight helped. "Dad's coming over tomorrow for awhile to put in some more lights over the new stalls," he told me.

That's when I noticed that the air was fragrant with the smell of new lumber. I managed to pause and admire the two stalls Dane had added that day, before I headed over to the area where the sleigh sat, now uncovered.

"Oh my gosh, this is cool. It's so pretty, even with all the dust, although that tarp helped some." The body of the sleigh was a bright red, as were the runners. I ran a hand over the plush cushioned seats which were a rich, deep dark red. The shafts that connected the sleigh to a horse were black. "I wonder how long it has been here and if it's still useable?"

"It looks pretty good—structurally at least—to me."

"Oh! I forgot to tell you...Sonya has the harness for it. I'll talk to her later and see what she knows," I told him, excited to learn more.

Dane didn't say anything. I wondered why. Could it be I hadn't taken enough time to praise his work? I reluctantly stepped away from the sleigh and walked back toward the stalls. Now there were three roomy ones in a row, separated by wood and wire in case the horses didn't get along with each other.

"You did a great job with these stalls, Dane. You sure work fast."

He gave me a half-hearted smile, and I realized he'd been pretty quiet since we got there. I wondered what was bothering him. He didn't stay long, saying he had something to do, so after he left, I called Sonya.

"So what's the deal with the sleigh?" I asked her.

"Come on over, and I'll show you the harness, and tell you."

"Okay, I'll be right there." When I walked over to the fence separating our pastures, I saw that Dane had already strung the wire the length of it, including the gate wire with a handle. But since Sonya's husband Bob hadn't built the wooden gate yet, Dane had left the wire doubled back and attached to the fence by the hook on the yellow plastic handle. I didn't know if the electricity was even on since both men were working on the fence at different times, so I left it that way. Besides, I still didn't feel comfortable around the electricity. The wire put out quite a jolt when touched, even though it pulsed. At first, I wasn't pleased to even have it, but besides being easy and quick to install, Sonya told me it was actually less harmful to the horses. Usually, one jolt was all it took to keep them away from it. Barbed wire and other non-electric wire fences could cause injuries, and wooden ones were easily broken, again causing injuries to horses. The one jolt I'd received so far certainly made *me* wary of it.

Sonya beckoned to me from the sliding glass door of her house's basement. When I walked in, I could see several long pieces of black leather, and some shorter ones with shiny brass buckles. "Here it is," she said, and then pointed out the different parts of the harness. "Those really long pieces there are the reins, those are the traces that attach to the shafts on the sleigh, that's the collar..."

"This is totally awesome. Now, tell me, how did you get it, and what do you know about the sleigh?"

Sonya's cheeks turned a darker shade of pink. "It's kind of embarrassing, actually. You remember I told you Justine was in 4-H?"

I nodded.

"Well, she admitted to me that she and her best friend, Aubry had snooped in your landlord's barn one day and found the sleigh. 'Course it was dirty and covered in layers of dust and cobwebs, and had probably been there for years, we thought. No one was living there then, so when she saw a car in your driveway and someone unlocking the door, Justine being Justine, she went over there and talked to him. She even told him about the sleigh and asked if it came with a harness because she wanted to teach her horse to pull a cart. He told her there was one somewhere, and if he found it, she could use it." Sonya took a breath. "Long story short...he found it and brought it over. It wasn't in the greatest shape, as you can imagine after all those years, but we cleaned and oiled it—several times—and Justine actually used it *and* the sleigh to go Christmas caroling with her 4-H group that year."

"So my landlord let you keep the harness? Why didn't you keep the sleigh?

"We didn't have anywhere to keep the sleigh. We kept the harness because your landlord didn't want it in the trailer since he planned to rent it out, and keeping it in the barn would dry it out even more. Justine only used it a couple times before she lost interest and moved on to something else. That's my Justine," she said with a laugh and a shrug.

CHAPTER SIXTEEN

The next morning, when I climbed into the truck, I looked at Dane and said, "You were pretty quiet yesterday afternoon, what's up?"

He looked away for a moment, then turned back to me. "Oh, I suppose I'm worried about Gramps. My parents went to visit him last night. They don't see him as often as I do, so they really noticed a big difference in him. They talked to the social worker and she's going to arrange for a care conference, with our family and the staff—head nurse, physical and occupational therapy, the social worker and either the on-call doctor or his assistant.

"What will that do? I admit, I don't know much about the nursing care side of Golden Valley."

"We'll find out how he's doing, if he's progressing as expected...I don't know..." he finished and looked away again.

I hated to see him so forlorn. I wished I could help, but I didn't see how. Maybe I could take more pictures of Misty for Carl. "Would it help if I visited him again?" I offered.

"Maybe. He's probably tired of seeing me all the time."

"I doubt that, but I could give him my perspective on Misty, tell him about her boyfriend."

"I'd appreciate that, Micah," Dane said quietly. He reached over and grabbed my hand. "Gramps really likes you, you know." He smiled briefly and squeezed my hand.

I squeezed back before I gently eased my hand away.

I walked into Carl's room separately from Dane as usual, ever careful not to be seen by other employees. This time, he didn't appear to be awake. I didn't have much time before I needed to start work. I walked quietly up to the bed. "Carl? It's Micah. Would you like to hear about Misty and her new boyfriend?" He didn't say anything, so I just continued on. "His name is Caleb. He lives next door. They like to eat together. Misty is the boss." I stopped, waiting for a response from him. When it didn't come, I asked. "Is there anything you want to tell me about Misty?"

He seemed to think for a moment. But whatever he might have said was interrupted when Dane walked in the door. Then it seemed as though half of his mouth lifted briefly in a smile.

"Hi, Gramps. Did Micah tell you about the sleigh she found in the barn?"

I answered. "No, I told him about Misty's boyfriend and then—"

Carl spoke. "Miss-tee pull 'lay."

"What, Gramps? Are you saying Misty has pulled a sleigh?"

"Hmm."

"Really? I didn't know that," Dane said. There was another long silence, and I started to say I needed to go, but Dane spoke before I could. "Gramps, I don't know what to get you for Christmas this year. What would you like?"

I waited, curious to hear what Carl would say.

"Miss-tee." He looked at me instead of Dane when he said it.

"Uh, Gramps, I don't understand. You already have Misty."

Carl looked frustrated, shaking his head back and forth.

"Carl. You want to see Misty?" I asked.

"Yesss."

Dane and I looked at each other.

Dane said, "Micah has to go to work now, Gramps."

I looked over at Carl, who must have exhausted himself saying those few words. His eyes were closed. My heart went out to him, and before I could stop myself, I blurted out, "I'll find a way, Carl. You'll see Misty, I promise."

Dane looked at me as though I was crazy.

I couldn't blame him. What had I done? Dane didn't even know the worst part. I'd made a promise, but in honoring it, I would lose my job.

I was so preoccupied with these thoughts, I nearly ran into someone just outside Carl's door. "Excuse m—" I started to say automatically, but before I could get all the words out, I realized who was standing there. Olga. *Oh boy.*

"Huh." She frowned and maybe would have said something, but I didn't give her a chance, I just kept walking to my office.

The rest of the morning, I felt on edge, waiting to be summoned to Mrs. Braxton's office. I knew Olga would tell her that she'd seen me coming out of Carl's room. As the day wore on, I began to think it wouldn't happen, or for some odd reason, Olga hadn't reported me.

But then I got a call from Mrs. Braxton herself. "Micah, I need to see you in my office right away. This won't take long, I have a board meeting in half an hour, so please don't delay." Before I could say a word, she'd already hung up.

"I suppose it won't take long to fire me," I muttered. I rose from my chair and walked to Braxton's office, my hands damp with sweat, and feeling as though I'd swallowed a boulder, my stomach hurt that bad. I was no good with confrontations, and had avoided them all my life—or at least since before my dad left. I'd dreaded the sound of their arguments, and when I was smaller, rolled under the coffee table as soon as the raised voices began. I knocked on the frame of Mrs. B's office door, knowing I couldn't lie to her. Not only did I avoid confrontations at all cost, I'd also been told that I had a very expressive face, which meant I couldn't hide the truth.

"Micah, can you tell me why you were seen in Carl Andersen's room this morning before work?" Mrs. Braxton asked me without even a hello, or have a seat.

My mouth went dry, and my throat closed off. I coughed and then coughed again and again.

Mrs. Braxton looked at her watch and evidently decided not to wait for my coughing spell to end. "I told you not to get involved in the resident's lives. This is a business. You are to get them in here and then if they need help, there are social workers and nurses and other caregivers here to help them."

"But I feel so bad. I've always been good with older people. They remind me of my grandparents, I guess.

The executive director frowned and opened her mouth as though to reply, but I hurried to explain further.

"They come to my office to meet me and then start telling me how much they like it here and what I should tell prospective residents, and then they stop me in the halls and other parts of the building when I'm giving tours. And pretty soon, they come to see me at other times and just chat, and then tell me their problems. I try to steer them to other people," I said hurriedly.

I thought of the tiny Greek woman whose son moved there when her husband died. He meant well, but he was too busy with his work and family to spend much time with her. She was very shy and her accent very thick. I know I found it hard to understand her, and often just nodded as though I did. I could imagine how much harder it would be for the other residents. Hearing loss made it even harder to understand anyone who spoke English as a second language. For that reason, plus her natural shyness, she had difficulty making friends. And she was just one of the dependent ones who came to my office or stopped me in other areas of the building. There were some with no family nearby. And to see their faces lit up when they saw me, it made it even harder to find some excuse to pawn them off on someone else.

"Hmmph," Mrs. Braxton said, and before the woman could say another word, Olga walked into my office and told her the board members were beginning to arrive. Mrs. Braxton turned to leave the office, but stopped and glared at me for a moment. "Well, just remember what I told you," she said in a firm voice and then walked out the door.

I breathed a sigh of relief. I'd been saved this time, and I hadn't lied—could it be Olga didn't know yet about my relationship with Carl and had only just seen me leaving his room? And I did feel that way about the residents. I just couldn't do what the director wanted. I cared about these people. They reminded me of my beloved grandparents. I wanted them to be happy, and if I could help them, I would.

Sometimes, I felt like a Realtor, trying to sell senior citizens on the benefits of moving to a retirement home where everything was provided for them—meals, apartment cleaning, entertainment, sociability, exercise classes, medical services, shopping and sight-seeing trips in Golden Valley's van. I also understood how hard it was for them to give up a home they'd lived in for thirty- to forty-some years, like my grandparents did, with so many memories and cherished mementos they had to discard in order to fit into a one-bedroom apartment, to leave neighbors and everything familiar and basically start over, often with people they didn't know. And like my Greek friend, often, they moved to be near children and grandchildren, only to find that their families were too busy to spend much time with them. Many people didn't care to socialize—they were used to living alone—and especially didn't want to spend meals with others.

Sometimes I felt guilty, that I misrepresented life at the retirement home and once they moved in, they'd be stuck there. After all, *I* didn't live there. I didn't really know what it was like in the evenings and on weekends, only what I'd been told. At least Carl was only there temporarily, and as soon as he was through with rehab, he'd be going home.

And someday, I hoped, I would find my kind of marketing job again, and I'd leave too. But meanwhile, I needed to keep this job and somehow, make one grandfather's Christmas wish come true.

Rescued by Christmas

CHAPTER SEVENTEEN

Saturday morning, Trish from the horse rescue organization came by, and I showed her the barn, the roomy stalls, and individual paddocks to keep the horses separated at feeding times or if they didn't get along all the time. If they did get along with fighting, there was also one big area of the pasture to graze during the day. I also showed her the large hayloft where several tons of hay could be stored. Dane had three tons delivered that week while he was there, which would get Misty through the winter.

We walked over to Sonya and Bob's place, and I introduced her to them, explaining that Sonya was happy to help with the rescue at the place where Misty had been boarded. We showed her their horse trailer and also Misty and Caleb, calmly munching away in Caleb's barn. As we walked back to my place, Sonya, who came with us, asked Trish when she thought the rescue would be.

"I think we may finally have enough volunteers, especially with Micah and Dane, you and your trailer, but since it's so close to Christmas, it's hard to get everyone together on the same day and time."

"Do you have enough foster homes for the horses?" I asked, not wanting to come right out and ask if I'd been approved.

"I think so. I need to get back with Leslie and see...can I call you later with an answer?"

"Oh. Okay," I said, disappointed. In my experience, when I got that kind of answer, it meant 'no.' I guess she didn't think I was experienced enough with horses. I heard a cell phone chirp. Mine gave a different signal, so I figured it was Sonya's or Trish's. Sure enough, they each pulled one out of a pocket.

"Excuse me just a sec, would you? I have to take this," Trish said and walked a few paces ahead of us.

I looked at Sonya. "What do you think?"

"About what?" She looked at me. "Oh, you mean whether you've been approved or not."

I nodded.

"She seems nice. I think—"

"Shh! Here she comes," I hissed before Sonya could tell me what she thought.

"Well, that was Leslie. Micah, I see you have three stalls, and we need foster care for three horses, but aren't you boarding Misty here?"

"I guess I misunderstood. Dane said you only needed another home for two."

"Oh dear...maybe I did say that. But we had one foster family drop out of the program recently..."

"Micah, if it's okay with you and Dane, you can keep Misty at our place with Caleb. She's over there more than she's here anyway. Just bring her food over at mealtimes," Sonya offered.

Trish looked at me. "Would that work for you?"

"It would be fine with me, but I should check with Dane first. Do you mind if I call him now?" He was probably out in the woods somewhere, cutting down a tree. I hoped he could get reception on his phone.

"Sure, go ahead," Trish agreed.

"Be sure to tell him you'd still be taking care of Misty, just next door," Sonya said.

He answered right away. "Are you just on your

way to get the trees?" I asked, surprised.

"No, been there and back already. Dad's getting the tree set up in the stand and Mom's already started on the wreaths. Has Trish been there yet?"

"Yup. Here now."

"Standing next to you?"

"Uh-huh. I have a question for you."

"Fire away."

"You know how well Caleb and Misty get along?"

"That's your question?"

"No...yes...just listen! "I stepped a couple paces away from Trish and Sonya" .Dane, they need room for *three* horses, not two."

"Oh?"

"Sonya said we could keep Misty next door with Caleb. I could take care of her there. Sonya said Misty spends most of her time there anyway, or she and Caleb come over here. The point is, I could take care of Misty next door, and still foster the three horses too. Do you think Carl would agree to that?"

"I can ask him, but I can't imagine he'd say no."

He paused. "In fact, Micah, just go ahead and say yes. I don't think this is a good time to bring it up. He'd just want to know she's getting good care, and that won't change."

"Thanks, Dane."

"Micah, wait. Does this mean they can get the horses out of that place now?"

"I hope so. I just hope they can be rescued before Christmas."

Trish said she would let us know as soon as she found out when the rescue would take place. They definitely needed all three of us to help that day. She asked what we needed for the horses as far as halters and ropes, feed buckets, blankets, and grooming supplies, and I told her I only had a few things that belonged to Misty. She said she would have some hay brought to us unless we could pick it up, and Sonya volunteered to do that.

Late that afternoon, Dane came to my door bearing gifts. He held two sweet-smelling fragrant wreaths, both decorated with pinecones and large red bows. One even had some tiny plastic horses attached. "These are from Mom," he told me. The larger one is for your front door and the other for the barn."

"How sweet of her. Hmm, they smell so good, "I said, sticking my nose in the larger one.

"I told her you didn't decorate for the holidays, and after she got over the shock"—he grinned—"just kidding, she said if you weren't going to have a tree, at least you'd have this decorated wreath. He handed me the large one with the plastic horses."Sorry, she's kind of pushy that way. And I know she wanted to do something nice for you and this was all she could come up with since she doesn't know you."

I felt tears spring to my eyes, and turned, opened my junk drawer and pretended to search for something. "I don't think I have anything to hang it with...a hook...or something."

"Mom thought of that. She puts a loop on them, and see, there's already a hook on the door. Want me to hang it up for you?"

"Yes, please."

"I can put the other one wherever you want it in

or outside the barn."

"Yeah, that would be great. I'll just grab my jacket and go with you."

As we walked to the barn, I told Dane what I'd learned from Trish that day. He stopped walking, and took my hand. His skin felt warm against mine. "Don't worry, Micah. Whatever it takes, we'll make it work."

I nodded and squeezed his hand. I thought how lucky I was to have this kind, gentle man come into my life. I wanted to kiss him...but I couldn't.

We walked in silence for a bit and then Dane dropped my hand to open the barn door. "Do you want the wreath inside or over a door?" We decided to hang it just above the doors, and as he nailed it under my supervision, he said, "The feed store is still open. Want to get a few bales of hay to have ready for the horses when they get here? I'll buy."

My first thought was to refuse, tell him I was busy, or some other excuse, but I doubted anyone I worked with would be shopping there. "Yeah, sure. But I just got my first paycheck. I can help out. I also want to look at their grooming supplies. Maybe I could get a couple items. Trish said the rescue organization counts on donations of tack as well as money. If these horses don't need them, maybe some other foster horse will. She also said they get some of their funds from tack sales."

"There you go. Good idea. Why don't you do that, then, and I'll get the hay. Are you ready? Let's go. "

I had another reason for going to the feed store. They had western clothing there too. I wanted to get Dane a cowboy hat. I told myself it was the least I could do for all the things he'd done for me, especially taking me to and from work every day. And now that I had some money, he still wouldn't let me buy gas.

When we got to the store, we went our separate ways. I headed to the horse supplies section, but made a quick detour to the clothing area and quickly scanned the hats for one I figured would be his size, 7 5/8. He'd left his cap on a post one day, and I sneaked a peek inside it.

"Need help?" a male voice asked, and I jumped. But it wasn't Dane's voice, so I calmed down. I glanced around and didn't see him, but I didn't want to attract his attention either.

"Can you tell me the price of that hat?" I pointed to a black one.

"Sure. The store clerk pulled it off the rack and flipped it over. But when he read the price, I gasped. "How about this one? It's less expensive." He pulled another one from a box and held it out.

Even I, who knew nothing about cowboy hats, could see the difference in quality. I would just have to do without something else I'd planned to buy with my first paycheck—like food, maybe. I hoped I could find at least one horse grooming tool or brush on sale. And I still had Mom's Christmas gift to buy..."No, I'll take the first one."

"Of course. Let me find the box for it." He rummaged among the boxes, pulled one out and put the hat in it.

OMG, it was huge. How could I hide it from Dane, I wondered as we walked over to the
counter. I glanced around again and then heard my phone beep. I looked down and saw that it was a text from Dane. "Meet me at the loading dock. Getting hay."

By then, the store clerk had put the hat box in a

huge white bag. "Would you like to put this purchase on your credit card today?"

"No thanks, I have the cash." I pulled it from my wallet, glad I'd cashed my paycheck during my lunch break the day before. Did I have time to look at the grooming supplies?

"Okay, here's your receipt, and...oh, here's your promo gift from the manufacturer." He held something up, but by then, I could see Dane's truck outside.

"Thanks, can you put it in the bag with the receipt? I see my ride waiting for me." As soon as he handed the plastic bag to me, I grabbed it and dashed out of the store, holding the bag behind me. When I got to the truck, I climbed in and stuffed the bag under my feet on the floor.

"Did you find anything?" Dane asked.

"Yes, I did. I found exactly what I was looking for."

Later that night, after Dane left, I pulled the hat box out of the plastic bag, and something dropped out—actually two somethings. One was a bright red plastic mane comb and the other was some kind of red plastic grooming brush, the promotional gifts for buying the hat.

CHAPTER EIGHTEEN

Dane had a small box on the front seat of the Subaru when we went to work on Monday. Curiosity got the better of me, and I had to ask.

"Oh, it's for Gramps. Go ahead and open it if you want." So of course, I did, and pulled out a six-inch tall Christmas tree with tiny lights and ornaments.

"Push that little button to the left." He pointed to the base of the tree.

And when I did, it lit up. I grinned, but then my smile faded. "Does this mean Carl won't be home for Christmas?" I asked sadly.

"I'm afraid it does."

"Well...about that Christmas present I promised him—"I started, but Dane interrupted.

"Listen, Micah, I know you meant well, but—"

I interrupted him too. "No, I have it figured out. If we can do it next weekend, before Christmas, Sonya said she will take Misty to Golden Valley, probably with

Caleb along for company. I also talked to Val, our nursing director. She said we could bring Carl right to the back entrance and the nursing staff would bring him out in a wheelchair. They have this awesome lift that they can buckle him into, and it will take him out of bed and into the chair. He won't have to do a thing. And our maintenance guys will put up those orange traffic cones and block off some parking spaces for the truck and trailer."

"Sounds like you have this all planned out." Dane smiled.

"Yup, easy-peasy."

"Okay, sounds good to me. I'll tell Gramps, my parents, and maybe some other family members. If you can pull this off, it will be the best Christmas present he could have."

If? What could go wrong?

Olga seemed more disgruntled than usual when I walked into the lobby. As I passed Terri's office, I stuck my head in. "What's wrong with her today?" I asked as Olga walked, mumbling down the hall.

"Oh, she's just miffed because she has to stay and

man the front desk while the rest of us go to the employee Christmas party." She stared at me when I raised my brow. "You're going, aren't you? You didn't make any appointments, I hope."

"Well, actually, I wasn't planning to. I haven't been here that long and—"

"That doesn't matter. It's for all the employees. And that's when the residents give us our appreciation gift. Yours won't be as big because you haven't been here a year yet, but still..." When I didn't say anything, Terry continued. "Micah, you have to go. There are all kinds of yummy desserts and Christmas carols, and Golden Valley gives us gift certificates to one of the local grocery stores...You're going. I'll come and get you at noon. Now shoo, and get whatever work that needs to be done before then."

True to her word, Terri showed up at my office, and I reluctantly went with her to the party in the basement. And it was fun. I graciously accepted the envelope with cash, my share of the residents' generous gift, that Mrs. Braxton handed to me. And when I got back to my office afterward, I opened the envelope to find a twenty-five dollar gift certificate to the nearby grocery store—that I could walk to on my lunch break—and three fifty dollar bills, much more than I'd expected.

Tomorrow, I would skip lunch and walk over to the strip mall nearby and look for something special for my mom. I should have my car back by then and I could make the drive to Seattle for Christmas.

That night, I got a call from Sonya. "Trish called and asked me to let you know too. It looks as though we can get the horses this weekend. I didn't know what to say. What time are we planning to go to Golden Valley on Saturday?"

"I told everyone we'd be there at noon. The nurses will have Carl ready then. What day is the horse rescue?"

"Trish said she'd let me know, but probably Saturday, because several of the volunteers have church on Sunday."

"Oh boy...well, I'll see if I can get Carl's visit changed to Sunday, but Dane's family usually goes to church too, and, I don't know who else will be affected by this. "

Why did this have to happen? I didn't know if the horses could be rescued without our help and Sonya's trailer, but I'd promised Carl he'd see Misty. I hadn't expected it to be on the same day.

I called Dane and told him what was happening. I heard a long sigh on the other end of the phone line. "I'm sorry, Micah. We have to get the horses out of that place, I agree, but you know, this could be Gramps's last Christmas," he said solemnly. "Not to put any pressure on you, but I just want to know that we did all that we could to make it a good one for him. Seeing Misty, well"—he stopped for a moment, but I'd heard the sadness in his voice—"you just do what you have to do."

I went to work the next day feeling just plain glum. Dane didn't seem to want to talk, but he did ask, "Did you hear back from Trish last night?

I shook my head, and we rode the rest of the way in silence. I put on my happy face the best I could when I had to talk to anyone, but it was an effort. I didn't even feel like shopping for Mom's gift, but I made myself go anyway. I figured the walk in the brisk air would help. I didn't mind missing lunch, I didn't feel like eating anyway. Nothing I saw as I browsed the shops appealed to me, and when my half hour was almost up, I decided to buy a couple hardback books, current releases by authors she liked. One of them was even autographed. I just hoped she hadn't read them already. Mom was a voracious reader, and especially when it came to her favorite authors.

The rest of the day dragged by. I still had no news for Dane from Trish when he came to pick me up at work that evening. "However, I do have some good news. The auto body shop called and said my car will be ready on Friday. Would you mind giving me a ride there?" He didn't answer. "Dane? Earth to Dane..." I teased him.

"Sorry, what did you need?"

It sounded like he was angry. What had *I* done? Maybe I should just ask Terri or Sonya. "Um, nothing."

"No, you asked me a question. What was it?" Now he sounded irritated.

"Oh, I...asked if you could give me a ride, but it's out of your way and I'll just ask Ter—"

"I'll take you. Why wouldn't I? So, now that

you're getting your car back, you don't need me, is that it?"

He *really* sounded angry now. Well, I didn't like his attitude. I was under a lot of stress and I didn't need this.

"Dane, we talked about this before. I *asked* you if you would think I was taking advantage of you, if you took me to work and back every day, remember? Are you saying now that your answer was a lie?"

"No! Oh, just forget it. I don't want to talk about this, okay?

"Fine."

We sat in stony silence the rest of the way home and I shut the car door harder than necessary when I got out. Dane remained in the car with the motor running, but lowered the window on the passenger side, even though it was terribly cold outside. "You don't need to ask Terri for a ride on Friday to get your car. I'll take you." And with that, he drove off.

Actually, another good thing happened that day to offset the bad. Sonya texted that she had something for me and she'd see me when we fed the horses in

Caleb's barn at five o'clock. I'd given up even attempting to feed Misty in her own stall at my place, and really, what was the point since she'd soon be moving out of it to make way for the foster horses?

I changed into my sweats and boots and walked outside with a flashlight, and apples, stopping to grab a flake of hay on the way next door. Misty nickered when she saw me and came over for her apple as soon as I walked through the open gate. I saw the light in Caleb's barn go on, and then a thump as Sonya dropped Caleb's flake into his feed trough.

"Hi," I said to her.

"Hey, come on over to the house. I have it just inside the door."

When we got there, she opened the sliding door, picked up the big box and handed it to me. "Is this the harness?" I asked her, surprised.

"Yeah. I cleaned and oiled it again."

"Doesn›t Justine want to keep it?"

"No, she doesn't have time to teach Caleb how to pull a sleigh, or anything else."

"Oh. I thought he knew how." I looked at her,

puzzled.

"No, that was her first horse, Bobby. But she said she›d be happy to show you how to use the harness since Misty does."

"Wow. That would be great. Thanks, Sonya. Maybe I'll take her up on that offer while she's home on vacation. That sounds like fun."

Sonya called me at work Wednesday afternoon.

"Trish just called. We're doing the rescue Saturday at noon. Does that still work for you and Dane?"

I tried to just feel happy that the horses would finally be rescued. "Oh boy. Can you still bring Misty here on Sunday?" I needed to know that first before I attempted to rearrange the day scheduled for her visit with Carl.

"Yes, that will be fine. Still at noon?"

"I think so. Thanks *so* much, Sonya. You're one in a million."

Next, I called Dane and told him what I'd learned. He said he thought his family could go to the early church services, and get here just in time.

Then I walked into Val's office. I wasn't afraid to get her involved this time. She didn't get along with Mrs. Braxton, which had become clearer to me the more we talked before I ever approached her about the idea. I was worried that one or more of the nurses and someone in maintenance might talk about Carl's horse coming to visit, but Val said they just knew it was something his family had arranged and hoped it would cheer him up. Unless Carl said something to someone, the only person at Golden Valley who knew I was boarding his horse, was Val. I hadn't even told, Terri.

CHAPTER NINETEEN

The rest of the week passed in a blur.

I was so happy to get my car back Friday night. It seemed like more than a month since I'd last driven it. It didn't even seem like the same car. But as happy as I was to have it, I was also sad that I wouldn't be commuting with Dane anymore. On the other hand, he had been so irritable lately, maybe I should be glad, instead of sad, about that too. So, why wasn't I?

Saturday morning, I woke up feeling anxious. I had no idea what to expect during the horse rescue. Sonya, however, seemed perfectly calm when we fed the horses that morning.

Bob came out too and backed the truck up to the trailer. Misty stopped eating when the trailer hitch clunked down onto the ball on the truck and dashed out of Caleb's stall, where she'd been helping herself to his food. Normally unflappable Caleb threw up his head and followed her, snorting. "It's okay, kids, calm down," Sonya said to them in a soothing tone.

I thought Dane would ride with us, but he said he'd meet us at the site with his company's pickup so he could help haul whatever items the owners were sending with the horses. At least it was not supposed to be a hostile removal. The owners knew they could no longer take care of these horses and had relinquished them.

Still, it was an upsetting time for all of us. The horses, who were being chased, caught and handled by people they didn't know, and then loaded into unfamiliar trailers, and for me to see up close what bad shape these poor horses were in. I heard comments from other volunteers as well. Some horses had what Trish called "rain rot" from standing out in the rain and others had "mud fever," from standing in deep mud. Several had cuts from trying to reach under the wire fences for weeds and grass. All of them were way too thin. But now at least, they would have a good life, taken care of as they deserved to be and someday find a loving home.

And, they were rescued by Christmas. It was such a good feeling to see the three horses munching away in my barn, standing in stalls with clean, fragrant shavings, I could barely tear myself away from them to go to bed that night.

I walked out the barn door, turning to close it behind me, when I felt a drop on my cheek. I looked up, wondering where it had come from. I hadn't heard anything about rain in the forecast. In fact, it was too cold for rain. Then another drop, and then another...something was falling from the sky..."Snow! We can't have snow!"

I hurried into the house and looked at my smartphone weather app. What! It showed a chance of snow. Chance? It *was* snowing. I looked at the time. Too late to call Sonya, she went to bed early. Dane? No, what could he do about it? Better to wait for morning and see if it stuck. Hopefully, these were just light flurries, and they would be gone by morning.

I had a terrible time sleeping that night. I kept getting up to look out the window. The snow hadn't stopped. I finally fell asleep, exhausted.

My ringing phone woke me Sunday morning.

"Micah, have you looked outside this morning?" Sonya asked.

"Not yet. Is it bad?" I stood, walked to the window and raised the blinds. "Oh nooo..." I groaned. The ground was covered. Snow everywhere.

"Yeah. The horses seem to be enjoying it," Sonya said drily.

I heard a squeal, and two of the three foster horses were cavorting in the snow, while the third pawed at it. At least they were having fun, and with the good food and warm barn, they'd found some energy.

"Maybe it will melt before we leave," I said hopefully, desperately.

"Uh-huh," Sonya replied in a doubtful tone of voice. I couldn't blame her. Just because I wanted something so bad, didn't mean it would happen.

"I guess we'll just have to wait and see, then. Do you know if it's just like this up on this hill? Maybe there isn't much snow down in the valley."

"Micah, I can't take the trailer out in this weather. I wouldn't want to risk something happening to Misty and Caleb, would you?"

"No, you're right...it's just that I *promised* Carl."

"I know, hon, and I'm sorry."

My next call was from Dane. "Micah, we can be thankful this didn't happen yesterday," he said and I knew he was trying to console me. He knew how badly I wanted to give Carl this Christmas gift today.

"Yes, that's true," I said dully, though I was grateful for that.

"Maybe we could bring her to see him after Christmas."

"I suppose."

"It's not your fault."

"Okay. Well, I'll talk to you later and let you know for sure. I need to go out and feed the horses now." I ended the phone call, put on a couple layers of clothing and went outside.

When I carried Misty's hay next door, I saw that Justine was feeding Caleb. "Hey," she said when I'd crunched through the snow to their barn. "Mom told me about your plans. That's a bummer. But hey, I have an idea," she said excitedly. "I know how you can still get

Misty there."

I doubted it but politely listened to her.

"Mom said she gave you the harness, right?"

I nodded.

"And she said that Misty can pull a sleigh, so..."

"But I don't know anything about driving a horse."

"I do."

I stared at her. What a crazy idea. It couldn't possibly work...Could it?

"Let's ask your mom what she thinks," I finally said.

"Bring the harness over. We'll put it on her and see how she handles it. Carl didn't say when or how many times she pulled a sleigh, did he? "Sonya asked . I'd been surprised that she agreed with Justine. But I hadn't known Sonya very long, and when I moved in, Justine was going to school at Washington State University in Pullman, studying to become a veterinarian.

I shook my head. "It's hard for him to talk," I explained.

Misty didn't seem to mind when Justine slipped the harness over her back, or protest too much when she buckled it on. With the new horses in her barn, who might not be her best pals, since she'd been kept in a paddock by herself, we decided to bring the sleigh to her rather than take her to it. First, we had to get it out of the barn. Sonya enlisted Bob's help for that.

The four of us pushed and pulled it out of the barn—no easy feat since Bob estimated it weighed maybe 800 pounds—but once we got it on the snow, it glided smoothly. Misty and Caleb both snorted when we pulled it into the yard, but she'd finished eating so at least we didn›t have to argue with her about that. Justine backed her between the shafts and had her stand there for awhile, then attached the traces of the harness to the shafts.

"Everybody ready?" Justine asked. Sonya and I nodded, and Justine coaxed Misty to move forward. First, she seemed a little startled, glancing back at the thing that followed so close behind her, but then she settled down and acted as though it was no big deal. So Justine had me hold the bridle while she climbed onto the driver's seat. Then with a couple clicks with her tongue, a soft flap of the long reins on Misty's back and a "Giddyup," she drove Misty around the pasture. Because that went so well, she drove through the wide gate, out of the pasture and out onto the road aways. No other vehicles had ventured out, so they had the road to themselves. I looked over at Sonya, and I think her smile must have been as wide as mine. She gave me a thumbs up.

Justine turned Misty around and came back.

"So, what do you think?" her mother asked.

"I say, let's go for it. Call your people, Micah, and tell them you're on your way!"

Sonya found a heavy blanket for the sleigh to keep me warm, and I bundled up under it in the seat behind the driver's, where there was only room for Justine in her long waterproof duster. To keep the snow from balling up into ice under her hooves, Justine greased the bottoms of Misty's feet with shortening, and then put the can on the floorboards at my feet in case she needed to do it again. Misty balked a little bit at first about leaving Caleb, but she was soon distracted by the new sights of the countryside covered in snow and concentrated on walking and then trotting through it. It was a much better route, than the one I had taken to Golden Valley my first day of work, and quite awhile after that. It wasn't until Dane and I followed Sonya back from picking up Misty, that we learned there was an alternate route. It might be longer in miles, but a much gentler, gradual slope off our hill and down into the valley.

The snow fell softly in big fluffy flakes that blanketed the grass, and the runners swished over the snow-covered ground. As wonderful as it was, I couldn't help wishing that Dane was there beside me. I imagined the two of us snuggled under the blanket, cuddled up, holding hands. What could be more romantic?

But it was just a dream. I'd lost any chance at having a romantic relationship with him and it was all for naught. I was going to lose my job anyway.

When we arrived outside Golden Valley, I could see through the windows of the closed back door, that residents and staff waited for us just inside. Then the door opened and they came outside, though not as many as I'd originally pictured. It was probably just too cold for most people. I was actually a bit relieved, since I didn't know how Misty would react to a crowd, and might be skittish. But she handled it like a pro, calmly standing while residents walked over the cleared sidewalk to her, using their canes and walkers. They petted her, while staff took their pictures. Strangers walking by, seemed startled to see a horse and sleigh, and came up to us too. I held onto the bridle while Justine settled a light horse blanket over Misty's steaming body, and gave her some water to drink, a little bit at a time. While I stood there, I scanned the group for Dane and his family. I felt disappointed that he wasn't there to greet us, but realized all of the family were probably with Carl, waiting to bring him out until we got there.

The door opened again, and I saw Chip walk out. As he turned and held the door, I saw a wheelchair with Carl in it, bundled up in warm clothes with a blanket across his lap. Dane was pushing the chair, and several people walked behind them.

"Dad," I heard Chip say. "Look who's here."

Carl looked up and saw Misty, and as much as he could, smiled.

Dane quickly wheeled him over to the curb.

Misty reached down and her big, soft nose sniffed him all over, as though she wanted to make sure it was really him. And if it could, Carl's smile appeared to grow even bigger.

Tears came to my eyes. I turned my head away, and searched for a Kleenex in my coat pocket. When I pulled it out, I first dabbed at my nose—as though the cold air was making it run—and then at my eyes. But in grabbing the tissue, I also discovered a forgotten apple. I brought it from my pocket and showed it to Carl.

"Would you like to give Misty this?" When he nodded, I handed it to him. He slowly extended his hand to Misty, and I heard a couple gasps from the crowd. But Misty took it gently from him.

I looked up again, and could see that it was an emotional time for all of his family, most of whom had tears in their eyes. I suspected it was emotional for others as well. One of the nurses standing by in case Carl needed her, said, "I'm so glad you could do this, Micah. I'm sure it means the world to him."

I didn't see Mrs. Braxton or Olga. I didn't expect they would be there on the weekend, but I knew Mrs. B. would hear about it. I didn't care. It was worth it.

To my disappointment, after what seemed like a short time, Carl appeared to fade and told his family that he needed to lie down. This time, Chip stood behind the chair and wheeled him back to the door, followed by Dane's mom, Julie, his aunt and her family. Dane and his sisters stood in a small huddle outside the door and appeared to be arguing about something.

Justine, who had been drinking the hot chocolate from the thermos Sonya provided, and answering questions about the sleigh, hopped down from the driver's seat. "I saved you some."

"No, you keep it for the return trip. I have that warm blanket."

"If you're ready to leave, I'll take Misty's blanket off."

"We might as well—"

"Wait." I heard Dane's voice behind me. "Micah,

can I talk to you for a minute?"

I looked at Justine. "I'll be ready in a few, okay?" When she nodded and pulled her cell phone out of her long coat, I followed Dane a few paces away from the sleigh. Everyone else had gone back inside by then.

"I want you to know how grateful I am...how grateful my family is, for what you've done for Gramps today."

"I'm just glad it worked out. It was a wonderful reunion I will never forget. He seemed so...so happy to see her. I just wish he had felt up to staying outside longer."

Dane nodded, and then we stood there in silence for a minute.

"Well, I'd better go, so we can Misty back home to her warm barn." I felt tears in my eyes again. And not just for Carl. After this, I doubted Dane would come out—unless he had to. "I really liked riding to and from work with you every day, Dane. And whatever you think, it wasn't just because I needed a ride." Leaning forward, I kissed his cheek, then turned to walk back to the sleigh. But before I'd taken a step, Dane grabbed my hand.

"Mind if I go with you? I've always wanted to take a sleigh ride...and we need to talk. "

"Okay..."

While Justine removed Misty's blanket, we got into the back seat of the sleigh, Dane pulling the heavy blanket over us. Misty had all kinds of energy after her rest—until we came to the hills, where we helped by walking along with her until we reached the top. Then we climbed back in the sleigh and she took off, recognizing, I'm sure, the way home.

However he felt about me, I decided I could finally tell Dane the truth—the whole truth.

"Dane, I—" But as I began to speak, he did too.

"Micah, I —"

We laughed.

"Ladies first, " Dane said and gestured for me to continue.

"No, please...say what you have to say."

"Okay. Well, I know I've been grumpy and out of sorts, lately...It's just, well this past month, carpooling/commuting...whatever you want to call it, and this whole business with the horses and Misty...I've really come to care for you. I mean, I *like* you—*really* like you. And well, I thought you might...care for me..." And he told me that he'd really liked me from the time we'd met, when he'd pulled me out of my car in the ditch, and then offered me a ride to Golden Valley. He even admitted that he hadn't just happened by that day. His had been the startled face of the other car's driver I'd seen briefly when my car shot across the intersection. He'd seen my car land in the ditch, and came back to help me as soon as he could get his car turned around on the ice.

But sadly, each time he'd thought we were getting closer, I'd rejected him. And then I'd told him I was getting my car back, and though he'd told me he wouldn't, he did begin to feel I'd used him. But I'd been so kind to Gramps and the horses, he knew I was a good person, and it didn't make sense.

"What you didn't know, what I couldn't tell you, was I liked you back but couldn't show it, afraid of what you'd think, afraid of getting fired. That's why I turned you down, not because I *wanted* to."

"What? Why would you get fired?" he asked

increduously.

"You wouldn't know this, and I didn't at first, but Golden Valley has a no fraternization policy. Staff is not supposed to spend time with residents and their family members—emphasis on the family members, and especially dating-type relationships."

"You're kidding. How stupid!"

"Yes, but now you know why," I said.

"Yes, now I know why," he murmured. He moved closer to me on the seat, and said, "You know, it's pretty cold out here. Why don't you come over here and get warm?" He wiggled his eyebrows at me suggestively.

"That's a very good idea." I moved over next to him, and he wrapped his arm around my shoulders. We snuggled closer under the warm, heavy blanket in the sleigh.

"So, sounds like you might need a job."

"I believe you're right. Probably beginning on Monday." I sighed. "But it was worth losing it."

"I know a construction and development company that has a job opening for marketing coordinator—you know, for ads, promotions, public relations, stuff like that." Because I was looking up into his face, I saw the twinkle in his eyes.

"Seriously?"

"Yup. And I happen to know the owners. I could put in a good word for you."

"Really? You'd do that for me?"

He nodded and then lowered his head.

"Why would you do that?"

"Oh, I don't know...maybe because I really, really like you?" His lips hovered over mine..."Or maybe because I like commuting to work with you?" His mouth got even closer. "Or maybe it's because I want to be around you as much as possible...what do you think?"

"I think...what are you waiting for?" I leaned forward so our lips finally met and let him know once and for all, how I felt about him.

"Hey, you two," Justine called out from the seat in front of us, as we came up for air.

"Drive on, driver," Dane told her with a laugh and we shared another loving kiss.

Epilogue

Two days later, on Christmas morning, after brunch and opening gifts and before we headed north to have dinner with my mother, I walked into Golden Valley, no longer an employee. But I didn't care. I'd already been offered a real marketing job with a construction and development company. My boyfriend, wearing a black cowboy hat, had his arm looped around my shoulders as we followed his parents through the lobby and down the long hallway to see Carl.

He put his arms out when we walked into the room, and as Dane and his dad and mom, took turns leaning over and giving him hugs, I stood back, watching. But when they were done, he pointed to me, and said, "Miss-tee..."

"Are you asking about Misty, Carl?" I asked.

"Noo..." he said, and I could see he was getting agitated, so I waited.

"Prezz-ent...you...Miss-tee."

I looked over at Dane, who was smiling. "You're giving Misty to Micah, Gramps?"

"Yess..." he said. "Christ-mass."

"But Carl, she's *your* horse," I protested.

"M-mine...to...give...yours...now."

Tears sprang to my eyes. I rushed forward to hug him. "Oh thank you! I will take good care of her."

"I...know..."

It was my best Christmas ever.

Because now I had a horse *and* the man of my dreams.

The End

ADOPT-A-HORSE PROGRAM
...to help heal and rehabilitate rescue horses.

"Horses are the most abused/neglected animal, probably one reason being that they require more time/money to properly maintain than most people envision."

Adopt-a-Horse is a program of the Clark County Executive Horse Council, a 501-C-3 non-profit. The program was created to accommodate area horses who are in dire need and therefore have been relinquished to Clark County Animal Protection and Control.

They have been relinquished because of neglect, abandonment, or the former owners inability to provide proper care. The horses are then given the tools needed to bring them back to health and to an adoptable state

The program provides financial support for feed, medical services, farrier services, and professional training.

There are currently eighteen horses in the program that are being cared for at foster homes, a network of several homes throughout Clark County that will foster a horse or horses for a temporary period of time until a suitable permanent home can be found for the horse. The foster caregiver provides scheduled meals, turnout, grooming, blanketing, meeting with veterinarians and farriers at scheduled appointments, and general well care. Care items include feed, hoof trims, teeth floating, de-worming, veterinary attention, vaccinations, post castration care, blankets, halters and lead ropes.

The foster home provides the care and any additional services they provide is greatly appreciated. Foster horses can remain in the program until a suitable permanent home is found. It's very common for them to be in foster care for more than a year.

The program raises money by cleaning, mending and selling used tack, holding a yearly benefit dinner auction, and also relies on public donations.

Donations can be made on their website thru PayPal:www.adoptahorseprogram.org
or mailed directly to: CCEHC, Adopt A Horse Program, PO Box 65008, Vancouver, WA 98665.

Their sister program, Ripley's Horse Aid, provides assistance to Clark County horse owners facing a temporary financial setback.

About the Author
Marilyn Conner Miles

Marilyn began writing as soon as she could print. Her first career was in the transportation industry, working for the airlines.

Her second career was in advertising, marketing and promotions.

Currently a freelance editor, Marilyn lives with her husband and cat in the foothills of the Cascade Mountains in southwest Washington State, where she watches horses and deer and sometimes owls from her home office window.

BOOKS TO GO NOW

You can find more stories such as this at www.bookstogonow.com

If you enjoy this Books to Go Now story please leave a review for the author on Amazon, Goodreads or the site which you purchased the ebook. Thanks!

We pride ourselves with representing great stories at low prices. We want to take you into the digital age offering a market that will allow you to grow along with us in our journey through the new frontier of digital publishing.
Some of our favorite award-winning authors have now joined us. We welcome readers and writers into our community.

We want to make sure that as a reader you are supplied with never-ending great stories. As a company, Books to Go Now, wants its readers and writers supplied with positive experience and encouragement so they will return again and again.

We want to hear from you. Our readers and writers are the cornerstone of our company. If there is something you would like to say or a genre that you would like to see, please email us at inquiry@bookstogonow.com

Made in the USA
Coppell, TX
23 July 2020